SO LETHAL IS THE LILY

KAT KEENAN

Also by Kat Keenan

Through the Wall Trilogy:

So Fell Are the Fae

So Wicked Are the Witches (Coming 2025)

CONTENT NOTES

This book contains elements of violence, mature situations and themes, & implied SA. Please be mindful of your triggers before reading.

For anyone with a little bit of pent-up rage.

ABOUT THIS BOOK

She's a witch forbidden to love a fae, and he's the assassin murdering her coven. Together they'll commit treason.

Lily always wanted to do more than the menial delivery tasks assigned to her, and now she finally has her chance. The witch Matriarch has chosen her for a secret assignment, one that is imperative to the future safety of Faerie. But there's a problem. When she meets her mission partner, it's the fae who's murdering her fellow witches at the behest of the diabolic Summer Court Lord, and to her frustration, she's inexplicably drawn to him.

Thrown together, Lily and Rune are tasked with laying the breadcrumbs to avert the loss of magic in Cirrelea. Using items stolen from the Summer Court Lord, they've committed treason before they've set foot outside the court. With a united goal and through perilous adventures, trust grows between them, forcing them to face the truth of their forbidden attraction.

With the weight of prophecies and their loyalty to Cirrelea on their shoulders, Lily and Rune fight against fae beasts and the Summer Court Lord to achieve their goal. All while never knowing if they'll find a way to remain together when all is complete.

So Lethal Is the Lily is a standalone fantasy romance set in the world of Through the Wall and hundreds of years before the events of So

Fell Are the Fae. This companion story is perfect for anyone who loves enemies to lovers, fated mates, shadow daddy's, the it's always been her trope, and loads of tension.

For Wall's sake, it smelled bad down here. How very like the Summer Court — to smell of death laced with rose. I resisted a gag.

The Underneath was below the court; a literal maze. Somewhere I'd never actually been, only heard of. Rumors told of fortunes hidden down here, but I'd always assumed it was an escape route for the lord of the court, Galwick.

My instructions had been to meet Vespa, the Matriarch, in this warren. Yesterday, she finally gave me an assignment that wasn't delivering herbs to the court's apothecary — more like poisoner — Maven. I was to meet her here along with the Oracle and my partner, and then we'd get the full instructions.

She'd given me a stone and a tattoo, representing a fae bargain she must have somehow entered on my behalf with the Oracle. It depicted a dagger surrounded by lilies, and she said I'd know my partner by his matching one. Otherwise, her details were minimal. Now her voice rang out in my mind, all lofty and mysterious, *all will be revealed tomorrow.* Vespa loved her theatrics, but the thing that really set this mission apart was her directive to cut myself off from the coven. No communication. I was to wall off that part of my mind. A directed self-exile.

It was unheard of, but who was I to complain? It was my first *real* assignment.

So I stood here alone, in more than one sense, and I hated this dark, dank room within the maze of tunnels. Galwick's foot soldiers could pop up on me at any moment, and those interactions were never fun. The Summer Court fae were beginning to hate the witches even though we served their lord. Old bargains with old lords tied us here, and our services were getting more of us killed by the day. Our ability to lie didn't protect us when the fae wanted their secrets kept., and prophecies of our power, our strength, didn't help the matter. It festered and bred animosity.

My partner was going to be one of them. I knew that much.

The Oracle was choosing him, so I could only assume that meant I'd be saddled with a fae. Not optimal, but an assignment was an assignment. Judging by all the secrecy, it had to be an important one too. Vespa had me as one of her witches in training for years, always saying there was something bigger in store for me. But I was convinced it was because she thought I was too much, too loud, too flirty, too clumsy. She claimed the lowly tasks were to keep me hidden from Galwick's view. *See, she's of no importance, merely a messenger and courier, not a witch that holds too much power and is a threat.*

The smell tickled my nose again, and I paced the room that Vespa had circled on a crudely drawn map. Where were they? They should have been here by now.

Confident steps sounded out, and I threw myself against the wall by the door. It wasn't Vespa, and it certainly wasn't the Oracle. Both walked with a soft pad, and this was only one set of footsteps, not three. The hairs on the back of my neck pricked.

I slid the dagger out from the band around my thigh, flexing my fingers around the grip. The steps grew closer. Heavy boots ground the bits of sand on the cobble floor, and I steeled myself for whomever this may be. Surely the Oracle at lest would accompany my partner. Was this some foot soldier of Galwick's? If they caught a witch alone in the Underneath, a stay in the dungeon would be the best that could happen.

Just outside the door, the steps paused. A breath. I'd lit nothing in here. Vespa had made clear this meeting was secret. It would just be the four of us.

A man in Galwick colors — a foot soldier — lunged into the room, using fire magic to light the sconces. He was fae. Otherwise, I'd sense the use of witchery.

I had to gain the upper hand. And quick. Once he was under control, I'd figure out what to do with him.

I didn't wait and hurled myself at his back. My one hand pulled his hair back while the other held my dagger to his exposed throat. With my witchery, I harnessed the now-lit sconces and wove it.

He grabbed my wrist but held still as he noted the arrow of fire I held pointed right between his eyes. How fortuitous that he'd created fire for me to channel from.

"Who are you?" I asked. Vespa had promised this area of the Underneath was not frequented, but he wore Galwick's colors: black and red.

My stomach tightened as I breathed in his scent of leather and smoky herbs. I knew that smell.

My flame arrow hissed as it steamed. The man's water magic doused it. *Shit. How inconvenient that fae can wield all the elements, even if only one can be done well.*

His hand came up to wrap around my wrist. "Lily, they sent me."

No.

That voice. My stomach bottomed out.

I spun him around, pushing him against the stone wall, keeping my dagger at his throat.

It was Rune.

Not him. Why him?

Of all the fae to send...why the one that I seemed unfailingly attracted to, the one who always seemed to appraise me with his gaze. The gaze where I always came up short.

The one who had killed my sisters and brothers in the coven.

"For what?" I ground out. I certainly wouldn't let *him* take me to the dungeon if that was what was happening.

His chest heaved, forcing me to notice how I pressed against him. If I moved now, I'd let on that his nearness got to me, and it always frustratingly did. It made me hate him.

"The Oracle told me to meet you here. Gave me some things." He patted the small leather bag that sat under his arm. "They're not coming. They said we have to go."

I pulled the dagger away from his throat, taking a step back. "You expect me to believe that? To trust you?" I couldn't keep the venom out of my voice. He'd been a thorn in my side for the past two years. A stupidly good-looking one too. He turned all the heads, but he was just such an ass. Always there to watch me screw up and then say absolutely nothing. No empathy. No scrutiny. No nothing. Just a blank wall. Then he'd meet my eyes as if to say *I saw that,* and then turn and walk away like he silently logged what an absolute screwup I was. Because if Vespa only gave me jobs any witch could do, then that was the only conclusion I could come to.

Rune stepped toward me. "Give me your hand."

I took another step back, sliding my dagger into its sheath but keeping my hand on it. "No."

He rolled his near black eyes, the light of the sconces reflecting off them. His hand whipped up, snagging mine. With reflexes like that, I didn't know how I'd gotten the best of him. He had to have known where I was in this room when he entered. Scented me. Heard my heartbeat.

Damn fae.

Stupid me.

He flipped my hand over to expose the new tattoo on my wrist, and, as he did, it exposed his as well. Same dagger. Same lilies.

I groaned. He *was* the one the Oracle had chosen as my partner.

Vespa knew how I felt about him. She knew I complained every time I ran into him at the apothecary. Why wouldn't she have told me? Warned me?

I ignored the tiny voice in my head that said, *Because she knew you'd resist. She knew you'd likely do something to try to change the fact that this is who the Oracle chose.* As if anyone had a chance of changing his mind.

What she had said was that the one who had the matching tattoo was someone I should trust with my life, and they should trust me with theirs. We'd each be given instructions, but this meeting tonight? She was supposed to be here to give me those instructions.

My eyes flicked to his. We both knew what he saw in them. Acceptance, whether I liked it or not.

"She didn't give me instructions," I said flatly.

"You sure about that?" he asked with a cocked brow.

Wall, the arrogance just dripped off him. "I got this tattoo and a stone." As I said it, I pulled the smooth blue stone out of the pocket on my chest and tossed it in the air.

Rune snatched it. "Don't be a log-headed sprite! Do you have any idea what this is?"

"A rock?"

Something thundered in the tunnels, causing us both to jerk our heads up and listen.

"We need to get out of here," Rune whispered. He had leaned forward, and his breath stirred the strands of hair by my ear.

"What do you know that I don't?" I'd been led to believe this was a mostly safe meeting and hadn't expected any trouble other than the potential for dodging Galwick's men. And by the sounds of it, we wouldn't be dodging. We had the full force of his garrison coming down on our heads.

Rune turned his head to focus back on me and not the noises. I hadn't realized how close we'd gotten. "Because if Vespa and the

Oracle didn't hold off Galwick and his soldiers, then we'll both be dead for treachery."

My eyes widened.

Rune continued, "That's not just a rock. It's the stone of Cirrelea." He placed it back into my hands and watched as I slipped it into my pocket as a sheepish *oh* formed on my lips.

The stone of Cirrelea was a fabled thing — created before the Burning. Legends claimed it had untold amounts of power, but no one knew exactly what it did. Those tales were lost in the Burning, along with much of our history. But this was Galwick's. He'd kept it on a pedestal in his quarters, and I should have known that was what Vespa gave me. But I'd never imagined I'd hold the stone of Cirrelea in my human hands.

Now, not only did I hold it, I had also just slipped Galwick's prized possession into my pocket.

I swallowed.

It was treachery.

Vespa, what did you do?

I met his eyes, hating that it was him. Loving that it was him. If anything was treacherous, it was me, my heart.

"We should go," I whispered. "Can you sift us?"

He shook his head. "Galwick wards the entire castle from sifting in and out, including the Underneath."

And of course he would know. He was an assassin for Galwick, the very lord who subtly had our mages killed off. One here, one there. He could do it slowly. The human witch lifespan was considerably less than a fae's, though still longer than a human who held no magic.

The other fae courts may have turned a blind eye to the dwindling numbers of witches and mages in the Summer Court. Indeed, perhaps they'd even been appreciative. The Oracle's prophecies held one too many things about the danger of witches. Yet Vespa and he were allies. Maybe out of necessity. But even Vespa occasionally remarked that fae should be scared of us. As one day we would hold more power than them. Whatever that meant.

Yet we remained in Galwick's employ even as witches mysteriously disappeared over the years. There weren't too many ways to get out of fae bargains, even if they happened before you were born. Unfortunately, ages ago, the witches of the Summer Court had bargained for shelter in return for our services. They hadn't bargained well and wrapped their daughter's daughters into it with too many loopholes. Loopholes that the fae excelled at exploiting.

And now I was stuck with Galwick's top assassin, the one he assigned to off my sisters and brothers, or so everyone said.

It didn't evade me that perhaps I was a new mark of his.

Vespa wouldn't set me up.

A small voice in the back of my head said, *She would if the stakes were high enough, if it benefited the greater good.*

There was no more time for me to mull over my thoughts. Rune grabbed my hand and led me through the maze. Occasionally, we paused to listen. He leaned over, cupping his hand near my ear. "They're assuming we came to the Underneath to escape and are trying to cut us off from the main exit. We've lost them for now."

His breath stirred the hair near my ear, making me shiver, and I hated myself for it. I turned to speak back.

Too soon. He hadn't moved. His lips were right there. Damn this attraction.

"We're stuck then. What good does that do us?" I asked, pulling back so our mouths didn't brush.

"I know an area that can be manually unwarded. We can sift from there. It's a safety net for Galwick. He told me about it as an easy way for me to come and go. An easy way to not be followed. And I don't think they know who they are after."

I shivered again, but not from his nearness. This time it was the thought of all the witches and fae he'd murdered on Galwick's orders.

He noticed the frown of disgust on my face and pulled back.

I couldn't help it. The words came flying out. "How many times did you have to use it covered in an innocent's blood?"

His face turned to stone. "I did what I had to do as many times as I had to do it."

With that he dropped my hand and tersely cocked his head — a beckoning to follow.

I may have doubted earlier, but I knew what he said earlier was true. They'd burn a treacherous witch at the stake. I had the stone of Cirrelea — Galwick's stone of Cirrelea. I had a tattoo binding me to his assassin. And not just any assassin, his bastard son. Being bound to a fae alone was means to expel me from the court. I didn't think there was a time when witch and fae could be bound.

I wouldn't even be able to beg for mercy at other courts. So that left me to living my days in the Suhmmerials, a mountain chain within Faerie outside of the courts, where the rules of Faerie were fickle and harsh. Treachery or not, my life would be over. The only way out was to complete this assignment even if I hated my partner.

TWO

We approached a dead end. Rune summoned a ball of light to hover in front of his hand and kept walking straight through the rock wall. Illusion — glamour. I didn't sense witchery, however he seemed to see a wall but knew it was a glamour by the way he held his hand out. But if all fae knew it existed, then what was the point? Who was it meant to keep out?

I didn't have time to mull it over. The room was empty except for a chest in the center. Rune circled it.

"This isn't usually here," he said as he nudged it with a booted foot.

"Is it for us?" I edged away from the wall we just passed through. No need to be right there if any of those other fae found their way in here.

"I don't sense fae magic." Rune now crouched, studying the chest.

I reached out with my witchery as he must have with his senses, encircling the box. "No witchery either." I drew closer. Something was etched in the wood on the top. I knelt, tracing my finger over it.

A witch sigil. It meant flower. "This is for me. The symbol means flower."

Rune grunted. "Open it. I've got your back."

Never mind that those words from Rune did something to me, and I couldn't quite figure out if they repelled me or snaked around my heart.

But he didn't need to have my back. Vespa and maybe the Oracle put this here. I was sure of it. Vespa must have known that she would never be able to meet with me. She did this ahead of time.

The chest wasn't locked, so I lifted the lid on squeaky hinges. Rune jerked around, frowning at me.

Inside were several items.

A journal. A sack of food. Daggers, just like the ones I favored. Heavy cloaks. And finally, four small wooden boxes that I needed both hands to hold, all of them locked.

What in the world? Rune, rifted much of it, putting it within his inter-dimensional pocket. I debated if I should give him the stone for safekeeping, but I had no idea how far I could trust him. My thoughts halted as I lifted out a cloak. There, at the bottom of the chest, was a single glowing vial.

I really hoped that wasn't what I thought it was. A glowing ball of gold light could only mean one thing. My stomach clenched. We'd certainly burn for treachery now.

"Is that what I think it is?" Rune asked, peering over my shoulder, having not yet rifted the cloak away.

I nodded. "A fae source."

"Why do we have that?"

I didn't know, but my heart hammered away.

A shout rang out. Close.

"Shit, they must have realized we didn't head straight out." Rune said as he grabbed the vial and rifted it along with the cloak. We were doing this.

Without warning, Rune wrapped an arm around my waist and

tugged me back toward the wall. Black shadow tendrils erupted around us.

Armor clad men clanked into the room. The shadows from Rune prevented me from seeing them, but they made so much noise that it was easy to pinpoint where they were.

My heart skipped a beat, but soon it became clear they didn't think we were in the room. Stupid, since everyone knew Rune held shadow magic, but maybe they didn't know who they searched for.

Someone kicked the chest. It screeched as wood and iron scratched against stone. "They were here," said one man.

"Then where in hells did they go?" asked another.

No one ever claimed Galwick hired his men because of their brains. I stifled a snort, making Rune tighten his arms around me in warning, which led to me becoming all to aware of Rune's hand splayed across my lower belly.

I had no idea what parts of us were fully ensconced in his shadows. If I moved, would it show? Did it dampen our sounds?

My body warmed.

His fingertips dug in for a moment, but other than that, he was perfectly still.

I forced myself to pay attention. There was danger just feet from us.

Rune hadn't been lying. This room was a secret. And since they weren't familiar with it, they might search the shadows more thoroughly unless they weren't sure who they were supposed to find.

"They must have slipped out of here minutes before us," one man growled with another kick to the chest. "We'd better find the others."

Rune didn't release the shadows. We stood there with his hands on my low belly, drawing all my attention as their footsteps exited the room and trailed off into the Underneath.

Heat pooled, and I hated myself for it. Rune might be nice to look at it, but he was Galwick's pawn. I'd do what needed to be done for this assignment and that was it.

His fingers twitched as he breathed in.

Oh gods. Heat flared in my cheeks. And at least it pulled my awareness from other parts of my body.

I stoked my humiliation with how much I hated the man behind me, willing it to turn into anger, rage, anything if only I could forgo this one mortification of knowing what he sensed.

His hand slid to my hip bone. "I think they're gone," he whispered near my ear.

Blast it. He did that on purpose. I fought the shiver and pulled away, refusing to look at him.

The shadows retracted, disappeared before he walked to the sconce and twisted it sideways.

Rune beckoned me. As soon as I grasped his hand, he pulled me in close. Our heaving breaths pushed my breasts into him. Wall, save me.

"Hold on tight, I've got you," he said, and then I was flying, my head light. Pressure grew and lightened before I felt my feet on firm ground again. My stomach roiled.

"Apologies, but I must sift us again." He carried me twenty feet away, and then the sickening pulsing of pressure was all around me again. I clenched my eyes shut. And when I was on the ground again, I vomited. He gently pulled the hair away from my face as I emptied the last meal I had onto the fire-colored leaves of the Autumn Court.

"I need to sift us again. Can you walk a bit?"

I stood, wiping my mouth with the back of my hand, nodding. This time, he took us further away before he sifted us again. All to hide our trail.

He hugged me this time, and I placed my forehead into the crook of his shoulder and neck as the world swam around me. How did fae do this all the time?

When our feet hit the ground, my head didn't swirl. Maybe I got used to the feel of sifting, or maybe it was the biting cold air that nipped my cheeks. Rune hardly let me have a moment before he had us jogging away from the area. The moonlight highlighted our frozen breath in front of our faces.

It wasn't long before my body was racked with shivers. I needed that cloak.

"Cloak," I groaned to Rune.

He paused and pulled it out of thin air. "Sorry. Forgot the cold would bother you more. But I also didn't want to remain near where we sifted. In case they followed."

"Can they follow us from that room?" I got out as my teeth chattered.

He nodded. "For a few minutes after we left. Galwick has it set to either keep it open or it can switch back to warded after a few minutes. Since we had no need of heading back, I set it to ward itself again."

Galwick was slightly paranoid. Honestly, I was impressed he'd even allow one room where anyone could sift in.

I tucked my hands up into my armpits underneath the cloak, which was only barely helping me keep warm. Now I noticed we were by the magical Wall that separated Cirrelea and its fae from the bulk of the humans. Humans who were rumored to be well-versed in witchery, but who really knew? There's never been a known case of someone crossing in either direction, though some believe fae beasts have disappeared through. In most of Cirrelea it looked like a cliff jutting up from the ground, but in some areas it cut off the natural landscape, marking itself as magical.

If only it contained fire that I could channel from to keep myself warm. Alas, the Wall was made of a magic that I couldn't quite decipher. Not witchery. Not fae, yet it held a note of familiarity to me.

Rune looked completely unbothered by the bitter cold. He had at least put on the second cloak, but he didn't even hold it close to himself. The bastard fae probably kept himself warm with his magic and forgot that even a fire witch couldn't do much if there was no fire nearby.

I wasn't about to expend myself to delve down into the abyss of the earth to find it. The cold already sapped enough of my energy. May as well turn my thoughts to other things as I trudged along behind Rune.

Vespa knew we'd come here. The cloaks said as much. My gaze flicked to the fae man with me. The one who brought us straight here. "Why are we here? What is it that you know?"

He didn't break his stride. "The Oracle told me we had to visit all four courts. That you," he turned to look me over, "would have information on what to do at each one. I was to get us there. You would then know what to do." We kept walking as snow drifted down in large, puffy flakes. If it wasn't so damned cold, I'd think it was beautiful.

I stumbled over a branch hidden beneath a layer of snow. Jerking my cloak back around me, silently cursing the branch, I said, "Jokes on you then because I have no instructions. I thought I'd be meeting everyone tonight and learning about the assignment."

Rune kept walking. He didn't even glance my way. I was doubting he'd even heard me when he finally spoke. "We should find shelter, rest, look at what we have. I doubt they sent us off without instructions."

Icicles trailed down over the cliff's edge to one side of us, and a snow-laden forest lived on the other side. Behind us was pristine snow with no trace of us having just walked it. I loved being a witch, but sometimes the fae's ability to always use their powers was enviable. That and the fact that I only just noticed he'd been hiding our trail this entire time.

There were no signs of life, certainly not a sign pointing us in the direction of the nearest Faerie village. The wind picked up and showed me I needed much more than the cloak Vespa gave me to keep warm. "Do you know of a place?" Wall, I hoped he did.

Rune's face set in a line as he curtly nodded. "But you won't like it."

"I daresay if we can build a fire and get warm, then I don't care what it is. Just take me there."

Rune picked up his pace, muttering something like *don't say I didn't warn you.*

CHAPTER

THREE

"You want me to strip down?" Was he insane?

We stood on the edge of an icy pool of water. A waterfall froze in thousands of icicles cascading down the front of the cliff and mounded on top of the frozen surface of the pool. Evidence that even the winter court occasionally warmed up enough for things like waterfalls to freeze and thaw.

Rune stood across from me, arms crossed. "I told you, you wouldn't like it."

"No. I'll go in my underwear."

He raised a brow. "And have wet underwear tomorrow?"

"We can make a fire. They'll dry."

"But you'll still be wearing them." He pulled a face.

"Can't you just magic them dry?" I waggled my fingers at him, which was a bad choice. Too cold. I tucked them back inside my cloak.

Rune cast his gaze up to the sky. "I'm going to ignore what you just asked me to do."

Realizing what he meant, heat rose in my cheeks.

He tipped his head back down to me and took in my burning

face. I prayed he thought it was from the cold. "Here's the plan. We strip down. I rift our clothes away so they stay dry. I melt enough of the water, so we can swim into the cave. Then we get dressed again by a warm fire."

"A fire I can then use to dry my underwear."

"It could take too long. I need you warm and dry as soon as we get out of that water."

My feet were already so cold I could barely feel them, and yet, he was worried about me being too cold after the swim. "I don't understand why you can't just warm me up with your magic. Or give me a spark, and I'll channel from that."

He pinched the bridge of his nose. "I'll address both your concerns. First, unlike witches, our source can get used up. I've already sifted us both vast distances today. Several times. If I use it for every little thing, then I could be drained, and what do we do if something happens before it can replenish? I also already have to melt enough of this," he motions to the frozen pool behind him, "so we can jump in. Second, I don't think you understand how this swim will steal the breath out of your lungs. It's painful. You won't be able to concentrate during a vitally short time before you lose consciousness."

I chewed my lip, not liking that he'd made good points. "I knew you all had to replenish your Source, but it always seemed bottomless to us."

He grimaced. "Now you know the fae's dirty little secret. And one sign the Oracle told me meant our time had come."

By the way he said *our* I knew he meant *us*. I swallowed. I was committed to this adventure of ours now, so there was no turning back. Only moving forward. "Ok. But turn around. Don't look."

Talk about him always seeing me at my most humiliating. I wasn't ashamed of my body. I was strong and liked my sweets, but the thought of Rune seeing *all* of me?

"Pile your clothes by my feet and follow me into the lake. We have to swim down a bit. The opening is just under the waterfall.

Once our clothes are off, we can't take long. We dive in and go. The cold...well, I just told you. Fight it. Swim hard."

I nodded, the skittery edge of nervousness skating along my skin.

Rune unbuttoned his shirt before putting his back to me while he pushed his pants down his legs. Total efficiency.

My mouth dried as he revealed his muscular legs and even stronger — I averted my eyes.

"I don't hear anything. Don't leave me here freezing my balls off waiting for you."

Right.

I dropped the cloak near his feet and made quick work of my Summer Court clothes. With my shoes off, I jumped from foot to foot as the last item — my bra — came off. I dropped it on the pile and shoved my hands into my armpits. Rune grabbed it and it was gone, into his Rift. My teeth chattered harder.

With one powerful move, he dove into the lake. Dear goddess, it was a beautiful sight to see all those muscles bunching and moving.

I took too long. His head popped up out of the water. Those storm gray eyes scalding me. "Jump in. Now."

I dove in, ignoring if I'd seen his gaze rake up and down my naked body.

The icy cold water enveloped me, and just like he said, it wanted to steal my breath. Thousands of needles stabbed all over my skin. All thoughts ebbed except for one: pain.

He grabbed my hand, grounding me, and tugged me with him as his powerful strokes brought us to the rocks underneath the waterfall. He guided me through, hands on my waist.

The swim through the rocks was not far. I had feared a tunnel where my lungs would threaten to explode, and I'd be left gasping for air under water.

I was already swimming up and breaking the surface which Rune had already melted. He was hauling himself up and out of the water. I grasped a rock, my hands blue and my teeth clacking together uncontrollably. He stood naked in front of me, holding out a hand.

The thought of hiding myself didn't even occur to me. Too cold. Too numb. My limbs weren't working quite right, but he snagged the hand that I was able to reach up. I crouched in a ball as soon as the frigid air hit my now soaked body. My hair froze instantly. I was going to be encased in ice within seconds. Rune draped a cloak around me before spinning and lighting a fire which conveniently was a few feet away and already prepared with kindling and logs.

"Lily, come," he said as the flames licked along the wood.

I couldn't move, so he gently picked me up and placed me right next to it. I stared into the flames, relishing the warmth.

After a few moments, he prompted me. "Can you channel from it yet?"

Yes. I should do that.

I sent out my witchery. The fire in front of me glowed red. Harnessing it, I made a simple weave to warm the cave, the surrounding air.

We both sighed. But I knew the pain of warming would set in soon.

To distract myself I asked, "How?" as I waved at the fire, the cave.

"I've used this cave many times to evade the Wild Hunt and other nasty things. If I had business in the Winter Court, this was my base. I got into the habit of gathering and leaving wood here in preparation for my next visit." He held his hands out to the flames. "That first time in here, when I found it, was a doozy. Thankfully I hadn't almost drained my Source, but I learned the hard way to take off my clothes to enter."

The room we sat in was small and blessedly dry. With the fire and my weave now warming us. I channeled more, drying myself off, warming myself. Rune threw off his cloak and stood up. The cold hadn't seemed to bother him like it did me. Fae always seemed less bothered by extreme conditions than us human witches.

He rifted our clothes into a heap, and he began putting his pants on. I got a glimpse of how well-endowed he was, having been too numb, too pained to have any kind of appreciation earlier.

I reminded myself that he had killed fellow witches, averting my eyes with a sentiment of self-loathing. What was I doing checking him out?

"Like what you see?" he asked, bringing my attention back to him.

My cheeks blazed, but the hell if I'd let him feel like he had the upper hand. "I've seen better," I said loftily.

He laughed as he buttoned the front of his pants and slipped on his shirt. "The cave. Pretty decent shelter for the night, no?"

Blast. Of course. "Right. I've seen better, but this will do."

Rune smirked as he rifted a bedroll and shook it out. "You should dress now," he said as he busied himself with the fire. A pot appeared in his hand, which he then filled with ice from the lake we'd hauled ourselves out of.

I gathered my clothes, nicely warmed by the fire and my weaves. Rune kept setting up camp. He'd shown no modesty, but that didn't mean I had to do that. With my back to him and the cloak still on my shoulders, I pulled on underwear and pants followed by socks and my boots. But my bra and shirt were another story.

I peeked over my shoulder. He stooped over the pot which he had placed over the fire. I quickly let the cloak drop and slid my bra over my arms. The hairs on the back of my neck trembled. As I hooked the bra together, I glanced his way. He jerked to face the fire again, and my belly swooped. Goosebumps stole over my skin and a shiver crawled up my back. That I was pleased that he'd been watching was something I'd examine later, especially since this attraction needed to stop.

Rune sat on his bedroll on top of a bed of leaves. He'd worked hard to make this a safe spot for himself. But of course, he must come here often. Galwick wanted nothing less than to end the Winter Court. Something about Lord Kieran stealing a woman from him when they were younger. I rolled my eyes. Men. Human or fae, they had that in common.

Rune patted the area beside him.

It was there or on the cold stone floor. So I sat down beside him.

"Dinner will be awhile. Let's look at what Vespa left us in that chest." He rifted the journal and handed it to me. Ever so gently, he placed the fae source vial on the ground.

"We know what that is. Why don't you keep that in the Rift until we need it?" It freaked me out to have it laying about. What if the glass vial broke? Then what? It was a fae source, and I was a witch. If I was found with that anywhere within ten feet of me, I'd burn at the stake.

I opened the journal as Rune rifted away the vial. Vespa's handwriting greeted me. A quick flip through showed another script as well. The Oracle's? Had they known they'd have to instruct us this way and not in person?

Rune leaned in. I flipped a few more pages. Blank. It was only a few pages. My heart sank.

I went back to page one where Vespa greeted me.

You both are probably wondering what to do. Cold caves have a way of unsettling one's spirits.

We are glad to see you are safe and looking for instructions. This journal is spelled. Empty pages won't be empty for long, but it ensures that information won't get into the hands of those who seek you out right now as you read.

Complete a task. Check the journal.

It is of the utmost importance that you both understand the necessity for you to succeed. The fate of Cirrelea is in your hands, and there are those who want to stop you. They don't understand what is happening to Cirrelea. They want to pretend it's fake. They only want to use prophecy and the Fates when it suits them, when it empowers them.

We can't allow this to happen. All of Faerie deserves to be saved from this apocalypse. An apocalypse that we already see signs for. It comes. The magic of Cirrelea will fade, the courts will cease to be, and those in power will fight until there is only one left. But will they be the one seeking to restore Cirrelea or the one drunk on power?

Your task is not to stop what is happening now. It is placing the breadcrumbs for those destined to fight for Cirrelea.

Those who seek power now like to remain blind to what may happen to generations after them. They seek to destroy the tools, the knowledge of what is needed. This is what you must prevent.

But we are nothing if not realistic. If you are caught, this journal must not be compromised. Destroy it by whatever means you have with you.

I let the journal fall a bit before looking to Rune, my heart beating a bit too hard, which was certainly not due to his nearness. It had everything to do with the overwhelming sense of foreboding that stole over me.

"I don't like this," I said. He didn't shift away, but he met my gaze. But there was one thing, so far, that Vespa hadn't addressed. A witch and a fae assassin. "Why us?"

He shrugged. "There are things the Oracle knows no one will ever be privy to. I don't question it. He knew it should be me. He knew it should be you." Rune nodded at the journal as if to say *go on*.

I continued.

You have in your possession four small boxes. These need to be placed in each court along the Wall. They contain the information we speak of above. You will perform a spell to conceal each one. Directions will appear when you are in the location. There they will remain, concealed until the time comes for one who will be able to reach them.

It went on to list the locations on a separate map that fell out of the pages of the journal. Their magic must have hidden it. Once we've placed all the boxes, we should burn the map. That would be the signal for the next set of instructions to appear.

So it wouldn't just be placing these items as our only task. There would be more, but we wouldn't know until we finished placing these boxes.

Rune took the map and studied it. With a grunt, he said, "We're not far at all from the location in the Winter Court. We could be there tomorrow and then move on to the Autumn Court."

It seemed easy enough, but why all the secrecy? Rune crept forward and stirred the pot, tasting a bit.

He wouldn't be able to return to the Summer Court in the end. Neither would I. There was nothing about the stone in these instructions. Nothing about the blasted Wall's-damned fae source. Yet, both had veritable nooses around our necks if we were to be caught. Vespa! Why so cryptic? Why not just tell us what this was all about? Even with some of the information she'd given us, it only begged more questions. The magic here will fade? Did that mean the fae would die? Would witches be affected? And no more courts?

Rune ladled stew into a bowl for me and handed it over. We ate in silence, both lost in our thoughts. After he'd rinsed the pot and bowl off and rifted it away, he brought out two letters. One for me and one for him. "The Oracle gave these to me just before he told me to find you and get out of the Summer Court," he said.

I grabbed mine and read greedily. Vespa's handwriting greeted me again.

The first words were a warning to read carefully as the note was bespelled to go up in flames shortly after I was done.

Lily, I can't impress upon you enough how important the task is that lies in front of you right now. Rune is worthy of your trust even though I know you don't think it. He'll have to prove to you that he does indeed carry your best interests at heart. The Fates made it clear it was the two of you who should undertake this mission. I was as shocked as I am sure you are. Galwick's assassin never made many friends, but in the short time I have now known him, I am convinced his honor and loyalty are to Cirrelea, not Galwick. I think you'd be surprised at what he has to say about Galwick if you would give him the chance to tell you. I doubt we will see each other again. This mission will take you far, and a homecoming isn't in the stars for either of you. Nevertheless, I hope to see your face one day in the after-world, and I pray to the Goddess that day will be long in coming.

I put the letter down on the rocks, knowing it would catch fire all on its own in a minute. I stared at Rune who was still reading what the Oracle had written to him. At some point, he'd gotten up and began pacing on the other side of the fire.

A sinking feeling stole over me that my mentor, my mother-figure, was gone from this world. And she'd sent me on some mission without telling me everything, purposely withholding information.

Rune crumpled the note he read in his hand before it lit up in flames. After a second, he turned his hand over to allow the ashes to drift to the cave floor.

"Do you think they're dead?" I asked.

Rune's eyes flicked up, the fire between us glinting in them. He shrugged.

I swallowed. If the Oracle was gone, who would Rune be loyal to? I'd always known him to be Galwick's minion, but he'd already committed treason at the Oracle's call. But with no Oracle? Would he get rid of me? Go on his way? The stone alone would be worth untold amounts. It could even get him into the favors of whichever court he chose. They'd probably even look the other way with the fae source if they got wind of it. But with a witch in tow? My presence would throw everything into question.

The stone weighed heavy in my pocket. I was glad I had insisted on keeping it with me, but Rune could easily overpower me and take it. Perhaps it was convenient that he brought me to the Winter Court first. Fire was harder to find and much harder to dredge up from the earth without it being extinguished in all the ice and cold.

"I don't like whatever it is you're thinking," Rune murmured.

I didn't like it either, but something in his eyes sparked something in me. I had to resist it. "Then don't watch me. I guarantee there won't be much you like there."

He sniffed, coming closer. "You have no idea what I do or don't like there."

"You're right. I have no idea about you. I don't know what you're thinking. No idea if I should trust you."

Rune and I shared a moment, silently considering each other before he broke his gaze away and said, "We should get some rest."

The warmth of the fire and the food in my belly had a way of making me drowsy. I stifled a yawn. I stood, moving to the other side of the fire, freeing up his bedroll so I could bundle up in my cloak. Thank you, Vespa, for that foresight.

Rune eyed me with curiosity. "What are you doing?"

I stopped my circling. "Trying to find the least jabbiest part to sleep on."

"Sleeping on the frozen ground will have you numb in no time, even with the fire. No, you'll get in this bedroll."

"Do you have another one? Where will you sleep?"

His lips quirked in a lazy smirk. "I wasn't in the habit of taking another with me when I go on missions for my father. I'll be sleeping in this bedroll." He pointedly looked at the one he just told me to get in.

I pulled the cloak tight around me. "No."

He prowled near, hands rising to unclasp the cloak around my shoulders. "The ground is too cold. The fire will be coals at some point during the night. We'll both stay warmer in the bedroll." There was something in his eyes that caused a warmth in my belly.

I couldn't actually be considering this.

"I'll tie off a fire weave. Keep the cave warm."

His hands dropped from my cloak as he backed away. "Suit your-self." With his back to me, he slipped out of his cloak and into the bedroll with a contented sigh.

I huffed as I harnessed the fire and wove it around myself to warm the air as I toyed with the idea of raising the temperature so much in this room that he'd crawl out of his bedroll. Just like he was loath to use too much of his source, I was loath to channel too often and too much. I didn't need to replenish a magical source, I only needed to replenish my energy.

I could tie my fire weave off.

"Correct me if I'm wrong, but my understanding was tied off witchery was fine for things like illusion, but tying off fire? Couldn't that result in bad things?" Rune lay on his side, watching me. The flicker of the fire reflecting off his dark irises.

Of course, he knew exactly what I was thinking even when he couldn't see or feel me trying to tie off my fire weave. I still circled, trying to find a place to lie.

But blast it. "Yes, you're correct." And I hated him for it.

"So that nice little warm cocoon you're in right now...you'll have to let it go before you fall asleep? Because I don't really want to be caught in some explosion in the middle of the night."

Yes, yes. It was one thing if you tied off fire for a trap. The explosion was the point.

His gaze followed me as the tension in the cave grew. He waited for me to succumb with an annoying amount of patience. He knew I would. I knew I would, but I didn't have to like it.

"Fine," I said as I rose and unclipped my cloak.

Rune lifted the edge of the bedroll, scooting to the side.

I slid in, the fabric already warm from him, but I refused to sigh. He spread my cloak out on top of his, which covered us in the bedroll.

He offered his arm as a pillow, but I tried to put as much distance between us as possible, the fabric pulling taut.

"Staying warm doesn't really work when we're not pressed together." His hand curled around my hip, tugging me back toward him.

"Keep your hands in appropriate places," I gritted out as I reveled in the warmth of his chest along my back, his long legs twirling with mine. "I'm only allowing this so we don't both freeze to death."

"Of course. I'll take this event with me to my grave," he murmured.

Maybe he'd find himself in his grave sooner than he thought. My eyes already drooped. Feeling him behind me was intoxicating and relaxing. "What happens tomorrow?"

He adjusted his head, his hand coming up to pull my hair back. His fingers skimmed my ear, and I had to resist shivering at his touch. I wanted him to do it again which made me hate myself.

"Will I respect you in the morning, you mean? Yes." His arm came around me, holding me close.

I rolled my eyes. "No, you asshole. What is the plan?"

"We go to the location on that map. Do what it says we must. We're slaves to that magical journal."

"And Galwick?"

"What of him?"

"When do you fulfill his orders?" Because at some point he would, right? He was no longer beheld to the Oracle, and I was an easy target.

His body went momentarily rigid behind me before he relaxed again. "What do you mean?"

"I'm a witch. Easy prey. I'm sure Galwick has some sort of standing order for you to take the opportunity if the chance arises."

He didn't respond for a moment, but his arm around me was rock solid. "He has no such thing, but even if he did, I'd never obey that."

The cave marked on the map wasn't that far. That morning, after waking completely entangled in one another, we'd made a quick breakfast and left. Only this time, Rune made his shadows impenetrable, and we could leave our hiding spot by floating through the pool without a drop on us.

Most of the walk to this other cave had my cheeks aflame. Had he refused to do that last night just to humiliate me? There was some consolation that he had been naked too.

"We're almost there," he said from a few feet in front of me. The woods around us were shadowy and held a mysterious beauty to them. A light snow fell, silencing the forest. The evergreen trees had boughs heavy with pillows of white, and here and there a deciduous tree's branches reached to the sky, barren. Every now and again, some small fae creature would cause a drift of snow to fall to the ground.

It was beautiful, but I'd be happy to move on from the cold. Besides, all the courts were beautiful in their own way.

The Wall was to the right of us, and Rune dragged his hand along some of the icy drips that hung down.

"I can't imagine the caves would be easy to see. What would be the point?" I said. They were the first full sentences I had uttered to him after he'd gotten us out of his hiding spot. He'd noted the fury on my face as we stood on the shore. All he'd said was, "What? The rest restored some of my source. Sifting would use too much, but shadows keeping us dry? Worth it."

But I had to move on. For whatever reason, good or bad, we were now stuck together for the time being. His comment last night, just before we fell asleep, had held some comfort.

Rune stepped forward and then back, causing me to bump into him. He'd found something.

"I think...yes, this must be it. It's well concealed." He turned sideways and disappeared in between hanging icicles.

I paused, staring at the spot where he'd just been. He hadn't sifted. But then the narrow opening into the blue ice was clear. A passageway. Yes, this would be easily missed. And we were to conceal it even better.

I caught up to him where the passage widened. It twisted left, then right and back again. I'd heard one could get lost in these sorts of places. So far there looked to be a few alcoves but nothing leading anywhere else. The sun filtered in from that narrow passage, bouncing off the ice, illuminating it. Then the entire thing opened to a narrow room. At the back, there appeared to be a slightly higher area that sloped down towards where we stood. A small rivulet carved through the ice from there. Rune stepped over it, his boots grinding the loose ice.

"Check the map." His voice echoed within the cave.

I did as he requested. Unfurling the parchment, the magical dot that was Rune and I sat exactly on the X that the Oracle or Vespa had scrawled on the parchment. "This is the place."

Rune rifted the box as I opened the journal. Words appeared in the journal, letter by letter, and my mouth went dry as I read.

"What is it?" Rune asked, stepping closer.

I handed him the journal, watching him as his eyes flicked over the words. The only emotion he betrayed was a tightening of his fingers on the leather-bound book before his eyes raised to meet mine.

"We've already committed treason. Why not a bit more?" His lips quirked up on one side, but there was a hesitation in his eyes.

The Oracle and Vespa told us to join our magics. Witch and Fae. Treason.

It felt intimate. Whenever I joined magic with other witches, there was a connection on some deep soul level. The thought of that with Rune made my insides swirl.

My hand trembled as he reached for me, his attention still on the journal as he reread the directions.

Rune grasped my hand, felt them tremble, and gripped my fingers tight in assurance. I drew in a deep breath as his gaze filled with understanding. This mission was truly in service to Cirrelea and no one else. Vespa had said it in the journal, in my letter, but I hadn't believed it till now. The Fates had a hand in this.

I sent a thread of my magic between us as he met it with his. What was a little more treasonous behavior?

Our magics touched, and a cocoon of safety and bliss enveloped me. I gasped. His eyes rolled back in delight, his mouth opening in a moan. And for a moment, we let our magic twirl and dance together. We played. Colors burst behind my eyes as stars whirled. And then a fragment of an emotion. A need. A want. A longing. And I swore it wasn't mine, but something in my heart yearned and commiserated with it too.

A crash outside alerted us. We hadn't yet done what we needed to do. It was as if we had the same thought. Our magics stopped playing.

Rune placed the box down, and together we placed a shroud over it in a dark recess of the cave. In time, the shroud would dissipate.

Outside the cave came shouting.

"Did you feel that?"

"Magic the likes I've never heard of!"

"It has to be them."

"Search the cave but be quick. That magic alerted every Wall-damned beast within the court."

Rune grabbed me, shoved me into an alcove and pressed his body against mine before his shadows erupted from him, hiding us from view.

Each breath pushed my chest into his. He held me almost painfully tight as our heaving breath made me entirely too aware of his body pressed to mine.

Footsteps ground through the icy gravel.

"Spread out!"

I leaned in to Rune, pulling myself up a bit to reach his ear. "Can't you sift us away?"

"They're too close. They'll be able to follow. Better to hide." His lips brushed the shell of my ear, and for a second I thought he hovered there like he wanted to do more. But that couldn't be it especially if men were right here in the room looking for us.

I curled my fingers into his fighting leathers, clinging to him. He smelled of leather and something smoky, something masculine. I let the scent soothe me.

Roars erupted from outside as the ground trembled beneath our feet. Ice rained down on our heads, and the footsteps came to an abrupt stop a split second before one of them said, "Shit."

Rune's body went rigid, and his head turned.

At least one man in the cave went dashing outside as shouts arose outside. Some were instructions, others were pure pain. The other man, however, crept closer. Stealth on cracking ice wasn't possible.

Rune peeled me away from him and pushed me into the back of the tiny alcove where we hid. His shadows muffling the sounds. The bastard was protecting me. Me! A fire witch. I didn't need protection from some Galwick goon.

Damn his shadows! They meant I couldn't see a thing. No doubt he could.

The next moment was a flurry. With one hand, Rune shoved me to the side as he twisted. A sword pierced his shadows, scraping the rock where my back had just pressed.

Rune grabbed the man's wrist with his other hand. The surrounding shadows morphed instantaneously into a rope that slithered around the man's neck. They thinned until they were a garrote.

Rune held him in a chokehold with his dagger pressed into the man's neck. "Try anything, and my shadows will cut straight through your neck. No amount of fae healing will fix that." He looked up, met my gaze, which was furious, noted the flames dancing around my fingers, and continued, "and for good measure, she'll incinerate your body, ensuring your head will live on forever in this cave until some craghorn comes and eats it."

The fae man, dressed in Galwick's red and gold, dropped his sword.

Outside, the noises lessened. The shouts of the men became fewer and farther between and mostly pained. The roars faded in exchange for snuffling, and the trembling ground ceased.

"Lily, watch him," Rune said as he pushed the man to kneeling. He kept the garrote of shadows around his neck. It looked uncomfortably tight as the man's Adam's apple bobbed under it as if swallowing was an effort. Rune used more shadows to tie his wrists behind his back. "His affinity is water magic. But he's not nearly as strong as you."

I picked the man's sword up off the ground and pointed it at his chest. Continuing to pull from deep in the earth, I created my fire dagger and positioned it at his groin, the flames blackening the leather. "Don't be long," I said with a sick grin. "Or maybe take as long as you like."

Rune let out a choked laugh. "You're lethal."

The kneeling man whimpered before Rune made his way down the passage. Shadows flickered to life around him before they enshrouded him.

The fae man in front of me glared. "Filthy witch. You *would* be with the Betrayer."

I snorted. "My, you all are quick. He's already got a name?"

"He already had it. His loyalty is to only himself."

My grip on his sword tightened. "How did he already have it? He was at Galwick's beck and call." Why was I even listening to this foot soldier? Even so, my entire body tightened at his words.

"Galwick has always known that one day his bastard son would betray him. Betray his land too. Seems like the prophecy was right."

"Prophecy?" I couldn't help but ask. Damned fae had a way of keeping secrets amongst themselves, even though the witches were always around.

"The bastard born of the summer lord will become the fated sword, which he'll wield and thus all betray, signifying the hidden decay."

My hand trembled, and I only hoped it wasn't obvious.

"Looks like the beasts took all your other men, my friend," Rune said as he ducked to avoid a low ceiling as he came back into the cavern. He rubbed his hands together. "So why don't we get to it?"

Rune squatted down in front of the man. "So this is how it's going to go. I'm going to ask a question, and you're going to answer. Truthfully. If you don't, I'll have my lovely — *lethal* — witch here singe you with her fire."

I repressed the shiver at hearing him call me *his* witch, not to mention how he put an inflection on lethal. He flexed his hands and the shadows around the man's neck and wrists tightened a touch before they loosened, causing a grunt from him.

"Why is Galwick after us?"

The man stared at Rune, then scoffed. "You've run off with the stone of Cirrelea and stolen the fae source of one of his bride's."

I swallowed my reaction. We were holding the fae source of whom? *Oh. Goddess.*

Rune and I shared a brief but intense look. One that conveyed *this is not good.* The Oracle and Vespa had truly screwed us over.

"The Oracle. What has become of him?" Rune gathered himself faster than I did.

"The horns blew. The Oracle has passed. We await a new one."

"And the matriarch?" I couldn't help but interject.

The man's eyes full of hatred met mine. "Burned at the stake. And it was about time. Galwick decides what to do with many of the others. He's rounded up the life witches. They burn soon. It was one of them that stole Sereanna's source."

I gulped. Sereanna was a known favorite of Galwick's. But my poor sisters. They'll all now suffer in service to the good of Cirrelea.

Rune shifted. "How did you find us? What does Galwick know about what we are doing?"

The man sneered, and Rune's fingers flexed, causing him to gag and double-over. With spit dribbling out of the corner of his mouth and red faced, he spoke haltingly. "He told us to come here. He knew you'd made a hiding spot. He'd had you followed once." He gasped and Rune released the garrote a fraction, letting him breathe. "He didn't find your spot but knew generally where you went. We felt whatever it is you did. That magic. I'd never felt the like..." His eyes went wide in wonder before he shuttered his expression, and his eyes went hard and steely. "He says you're trying to tear down the wall."

Rune barked out a laugh and cracked his knuckles. "And why does he think we're trying to do that? That's insanity."

"You're not?" The man faltered.

"Answer the question." Rune nodded to me, and I let the flame from my magical dagger flare. The man hissed with a cringe. All the other questions, while informative, were just to muddle this foot soldier's brain. Now Rune got to what we really wanted to know.

"Isn't that what the stone is for?" he asked, incredulity lacing his words.

We didn't know yet what we were supposed to do with the stone, but they held untold power. Could that be what they wanted us to do? *Goddess, help us.*

I dropped the flames down to the normal level. "Is that what the stone is for?"

His eyes bulged. "You took the stone, and you don't know what it does?" For someone who'd just had his balls singed, it was a lot of moxie how much incredulity he put in his tone.

"Is that what it does?" I let the flames grow as I hardened my voice.

He backed up as much as he could. "It's one of the fabled uses."

My eyes flashed to Rune. "Did you know this?"

Fuck.

Rune's face was a grim line, but his eyes held shock. A shadow in them mirrored what I felt. Doubt.

"When did you know this?" I barked at the man. I flared the flame when he didn't answer.

"Wall, I'll never be a father if you keep that up." Tears now streaked down his cheeks

"Least of your worries," I said.

He hissed, trying to lean back as much as he could, but I only followed. "Ahh...." Sweat beaded on his forehead. "I only found out yesterday — overheard Galwick say it to Maven — but I figured if you stole it, then you would know. I swear."

Rune grit out. "We didn't steal it." His tone confirmed what I thought moments ago. We were pawns of the Oracle and Matriarch.

Because if they expected us to tear down the Wall...

"Lily," Rune said as he nodded at the flaming dagger I still held at the other man's crotch. I quickly pulled it away. Once it was away, the other man folded forward in a sweaty sobbing mess.

"What are we doing with him?" I asked. We couldn't keep him around as we disguised the cave.

The man lifted his head and spat with venom at me, "One of these days, I'll see you on the stake, witch."

Rune's eyes darkened. "Wait here," he growled as he grabbed the other man by his chain mail shirt and sifted away.

I stood there, dumbstruck. "Great. He just left me here," I said to no one.

Moments later, Rune reappeared in the same spot he had left from. Blood splattered his beautiful face in a slash, and a leaf from a Summer Court tree was caught in his shoulder-length black hair.

I recoiled. "What did you do?"

"What needed to be done."

Outside, bodies — more like body parts — were strewn about, steaming and bloodying the pristine white. Flakes fell steadily, already beginning to cover the bodies, an odd sort of fleecing of the violence that had just occurred here.

I swallowed, resisting the urge to gag. I'd seen death and destruction before, but these were shredded scraps.

The brutality of it only served to remind me of the killer I was now bound to, but I knew this wasn't him. "What did this?"

Rune's eyes cast about. He was cold, lifeless. "Craghorn."

We didn't have those in the Summer Court. I'd never been gladder to never have encountered one. "Are we safe? Will they come back?"

He slid his gaze to mine. Any humor, any faux friendliness we had found earlier was now missing from his eyes. The arc of blood was peppered with white as it froze to his skin.

I had to resist flinching.

"They ate their fill. For now. We should get this done and move on."

A tremble went through me at the monotone of his voice. "Right."

Again, the journal instructed us to join our magics and cast an illusion over the already hidden passage. It was like camouflage, changing over time and always matching the surroundings. For a time it would be impenetrable. We'd key it to a certain type of witch, just like the box inside the cave.

We each placed a hand on either side of the cave's opening and joined our other two. Rune was cold, his skin dry. At our first touch, a tremble went through him. *Don't think how this hand likely just slit another's throat.*

"Let's just get this done," I said, barely meeting his eyes.

His slid shut at that before he murmured, "We'll sift as soon as it is finished." He sent out his magic, and I joined his with mine.

We tumbled into the dance. The joy.

How? How did it feel like this with him?

As soon as our magic touched, we couldn't help but be swept away with it. He was exhausted physically. From the foot soldier, from yesterday, from years of being at Galwick's beck and call. Somehow, I could pick up on all of that. Our dance slowed, and we got to work. Even that was comfortable, soothing.

We worked together. I wove an illusion, and he wove the fae glamour right inside it. Our magics crossing over and under one another, becoming one.

As we finished, our eyes opened. Neither of us pulled our magic away. And then it was there. That feeling. The longing. The absolute sorrow.

My heart thudded in my chest. These were his emotions.

His thumb moved ever so slightly, a caress over mine. Once. Twice. Before his gaze flicked to my lips.

Heat pooled low in my belly. I wanted to move into his embrace — let him hold me. His lips parted like he was about to say something.

A roar shook the ground beneath our feet.

Our magics dropped. Instinctually, I dove my witchery deep into the earth, delving until I found the heat once again. I'd have one shot. The magic Rune and I had already performed and the fact that I'd already searched deeply into the land to deal with Galwick's man had taken a toll.

The trees swayed, branches cracked, and a white beast nearly as tall as the treetops came crashing through. Horns lay on either side of its head and one on its nose. White shaggy fur covered it, but around its maw the fur was stained red. It roared at us, a hoof pawing the ground. More roars sounded out. My heart was in my throat.

I did the only thing I could think of. I sent a fireball straight for it. Trees burst into flames. Rune grabbed me, and that sick feeling of being ripped through time and space pierced through me.

We crashed to the ground like he couldn't control the sift. Snow billowed as we rolled. A distant roar echoed through the air, overcoming the silence that the softly drifting snow created. Rune gasped on the ground.

The sift was too much for him. Who knows how far he'd taken Galwick's foot soldier. The leaf in his hair was still caught there. He'd gone all the way to the Summer Court.

"I tried to get into the cave…" His teeth chattered.

I crawled to him as I took in my surroundings. The pool of water; the cave we stayed in. He hadn't gotten us inside. We both lay a few feet from the shore.

Another roar. Those beasts were too close. We wouldn't be safe here.

"Can you move?" I asked.

"I think I'll have to." He groaned as he sat upright. "I'm tapped out. If I tried even one inch further, I'd have burned myself out."

Smoke drifted in the air. Too close, and they were utterly pissed off right now.

I started stripping out of my clothes. Rune sat there gaping for a moment before he began removing his. There was no chance of rifting them right now. Within moments, he stood before me, naked. His sword still strapped to him.

"Can you make it?" I asked, forcing myself to not cover myself. I'd be damned if I sat here ashamed in front of him. I'd bundled all our clothes into the one bag I carried.

His gaze drifted down to my toes before he nodded. I didn't stop to see his reaction to the perusal of my body. What it did to me was more than I could handle at the moment. Instead, I used the still barely lit coals in the cave to melt a hole in the icy lake and leapt in.

His splash followed. The water must have energized him as he swam past me. This time, he didn't aid me. I followed him through the underwater tunnel into the cave. We both popped our heads out of the water at the same time. Now we were safe from the craghorns, but a new danger was upon us.

I flung myself up onto the rocky side. Adrenaline, this time, aided me. The knowledge that I was the one guiding us meant I had no time to recognize the pain. Rune, however, was not ok. He reached for the rocks, slipping as he tried to climb up. I grabbed his arm, helping him. From there, I harnessed the fire again within the coals, praying it would be enough. That I had enough strength left to do what was needed. My lungs burned with the cold, with the drain of using my witchery again. But I had to get the fire fully lit and quickly.

Rune crawled to the bedroll as I strained, weaving the fire around the logs Rune had placed before we left. Thank the Wall for that habit of his. The weave slipped, unraveled, so I began again. Rune's strong body was utterly racked with chills. The sound of his teeth clacking together echoed inside the cavern. But then flames licked against the logs, and I sighed in relief before crawling toward the bedroll.

The logs began to crackle. Luscious heat drifted across my body in waves as the flames grew higher.

I only needed to try once more, and then the oblivion I knew was coming could take me. I dragged myself into the bedroll, so chilled I was heedless of my nudity or Rune's. Exhaustion stalked me, but that didn't stop me from knowing that a comfort stole over me as I wrapped my arms around a dangerously cold Rune.

He sighed as my body pressed against his. I wasn't even sure how conscious he was at this point. I channeled from the now steady fire and warmed the room. It would cost me my consciousness, but he needed it. I needed it.

Another soft sigh sifted from between his lips as his breath steadied. I cocooned the warmth around us, filling the bedroll with it. The skin beneath mine heated. His eyes stayed shut, so I placed my head on his chest and listened to the steady beat of his heart before I drifted away.

CHAPTER

SIX

Something hot and hard pushed against my back. Arms tightened around me. The skin to skin sensation was luscious. I shifted and groaned, nestling in and reveling in how decadent it felt. I was in a warm, floating cloud. Sparks tickled along my skin as a hand coasted from my ribs to my hip and then over my stomach. Scratch that. I was on a very hot, very sensual floating cloud. My muscles fluttered.

I wanted to stay here forever. This dream was everything I ever wanted in a dream. But it would probably end soon. Right as it got good. They always did.

I shifted, and a hand that was under my head drifted down to my breasts, making me moan again as the fingertips toyed with me. Oh. Yes.

Yes. Yes. Yes.

His other hand spread over my belly and headed down. Down, so close to where I wanted it to be. I shifted again, parting my legs with a frustrated groan.

"Will you be wet for me, Lily? How wet will you be?"

My eyes shot open at the sound of Rune's voice.

Not a dream. Not a dream at all.

His fingers kept gliding slowly down, as his beard rubbed along my cheek.

My eyes shuttered closed. Oh, goddess. My back arched, full of want. Need.

"Tell me you want this," he said into my ear before his teeth lightly clamped down on my lobe.

His words cleared the fog of lust.

Did I? Did I want this?

His hands had paused, waiting.

My body most certainly did, but this was Rune, a killer. He'd probably get rid of me in the end, too. If I let him in this way, then he'd place another dagger in my heart too, because something was pulling me toward him. And I couldn't seem to help it.

I closed my legs, turning away from him. "No. Stop."

He removed his hands immediately and rolled away. A chill stole across my spine. "I'm sorry. I don't know what came over me." He groaned, removed his one arm from under my hand as gently as he could. A scratching noise told me he scrubbed his hands over his face. "I woke up, and you were rubbing on me and your scent... I thought...I thought... I don't know. I thought you wanted it, too."

"I was asleep, dreaming. Let's just forget about it." I faced the fire, glad that he couldn't see how red I surely was. I pressed my thighs together, trying to soothe the ache.

Behind me, he didn't move. I'd never been more keenly aware of my nakedness. I sent my witchery to the fire, now only smoldering coals, and warmed the cavern again.

"Who were you dreaming about?" His gravelly whisper broke the silence, but just barely.

I didn't want to answer. I didn't know *how* to answer. Sitting up, I pulled as much of the bedroll with me as possible. The bag of my clothes and Rune's was close. My first priority was to get out our clothes, dry them off, and end this Wall-blasted awkwardness.

Water steamed out of them, raising the humidity in the cave. With my bare necessities dry, I slid them on quickly.

"Who?" Rune asked again, gently. Too gently.

It made me want to tell him, to be truthful that it was him. He factored into my dreams too many times to count over the years. Even when I was seeing someone, even when someone lay next to me in my bed. But that way lay danger.

"My last lover, if you must know," I said as loftily as I could manage. To turn the knife, I added, "he was the best I ever had."

"Landon?" Rune asked with a scoff. "He's a sadistic ass. I doubt he'd be good in bed. Unless you're into that sort of thing."

My breath caught. He knew who I'd last seen. I didn't want to let that part sink in, yet it did. It also sunk in that he was right about Landon being an ass. He was a selfish lover, entirely too pretty, and was a believer that his looks meant I should worship him. But sadistic? Other than some consensual light bondage, I didn't know what he meant.

I snorted. "What would you know about what I like in bed?"

Rune said nothing, but I could have sworn the ghost of a finger trailed down my shoulder blade. With no answer, I turned toward him. Finally getting the courage to look him in the eye after what had happened, armored in only my utilitarian underthings.

His gaze was on me. Intense to the point that I squirmed. His dark eyes held a depth I hadn't seen yet. Sometimes they could appear so utterly cold. "I don't," he said so low I could barely hear it. And then a ghost of a voice whispered to me, *but I want to learn.*

A shiver tore through me, and it had nothing to do with the chill in the cave, and I briskly turned back to my clothes.

What was this between us? I'd been attracted to plenty of men, both fae and human, but with Rune it was as if I didn't only think he was attractive. There was a sense I knew him, and he knew me. That if I just allowed it, allowed him to see me, then not only would he do that, but he'd worship and cherish me too. And, blast, I just didn't understand why, so I steeled my nerves. "See, you can't make that claim about Landon then," and with as much immodesty as I could muster, I stood up so I could slip my pants back on.

As I did, I channeled more fire and dried the rest of the pile. "Your clothes are dry. Do you have any of your source back?"

Back to business. Nothing to see here.

Rune lay in the bedroll, staring at the rock ceiling above. I tossed him his clothes, which he caught one handed before they landed on his face. At least our swim, as icy cold as it was, had cleaned that soldier's blood from his face. Although it would have been a good reminder to me.

"I can sift us to the Spring Court, but then I'll need to rest again."

"What about the Autumn Court? That's closer."

"Spring Court is warmer for sleeping. I thought you'd prefer it. I have some friends there. They'd shelter us. Besides, with Galwick's men looking for us, I suspect he has some idea of the task we've been assigned. I can't imagine the Oracle or Vespa broke, but Galwick has been working on some things. If he's been successful..." Rune drove a hand through his hair.

Sleeping...prefer. I tried to let that one roll off my back. And ignore the pang in my belly, knowing that our next rest would be separate bedrolls. Instead, I focused on where he trailed off. "What was he working on?"

Rune stood, giving me an eyeful, so I turned back to the fire as he dressed, squeezing my eyes shut. *That* was a reminder I didn't need. *Don't think about it. Don't imagine it. Don't* anything *with it.* I took a deep breath in and let it out slowly.

"Potions. Serums. Things that would make people talk, unwillingly, and for fae, more freely." The slide of his leather over his skin made my eyes flutter shut.

I needed to get control of myself. This attraction was too much. It wasn't normal.

The thought brought forth a simmering anger. Was he doing something to me? But if he was, then he'd been doing it for years. I had been drawn to him since we met at my first Spring Equinox celebration. After that, if he trained in the yard, I found myself stopping to watch even if I had places to be. Many of my delivery assignments weren't actually that bothersome. It put me in his path often. Galwick's apothecary was someone Rune visited often too. Likely coating his weapons for his next assignment, and I brought the herbs and plants needed to make those poisons.

Then there were the other festivities. Galwick loved his parties and many times he requested the witches attend, though it wasn't a request. At those, we needed to act like we were having fun "in order to appease any straining ties." Many drank the enchanted wine, which made you crave the touch of another. Any inhibitions about who could appease your craving were gone.

I always danced, never touching the wine. I'd watch Rune across the bonfire. He'd be somewhere in the back, dressed in black. Hardly visible except for the firelight flickering over his features. A few times I was tempted to pick up a wineglass even after I understood his job. So what if I lost my inhibitions and gave into a craving the wine caused? Never mind that particular craving was already present.

Neither of us ever drank it.

And he never made a move to help any of the other women, either.

So I would just dance, telling myself it was what was expected of me at one of these events. And stuffing down the blasted hope that welled in me that maybe, just maybe, he'd notice me. Notice me doing anything other than dropping my entire basket of herbs in front of him because his presence startled me so much that I fumbled it.

My anger ebbed away. He wasn't doing it to me. It was inexplicable, so best to ignore it.

"Truth serums?" The implications of that with the Oracle and Vespa... It could mean our entire assignment would be compromised. Fae couldn't lie, but they were masters at omission and deception. And he'd said "talk more freely"

"You handled deliveries to Maven? Did the herbs change over the last few weeks?"

I nodded, thinking. "My last few deliveries held a lot more primrose."

Rune chewed his lip as he shrugged on a shirt. I definitely did not notice the rippling muscles over his chest and abs or the sprinkling of hair on his pecs. "Maven must have figured something out, but from what I could tell, he must have just thought he had it and primrose takes a long time to distill." He looked up. "Hopefully, that means the potion hasn't been administered yet."

"You think they're alive?"

Rune set about prepping the cave like he had this morning. This time I more than understood and helped bring some logs over.

"I don't know. That soldier said the Oracle had passed, and that they awaited a new one. But..." His voice trailed off.

"But?" I prompted, as I used my magic to put out the fire, leaving a few coals. I'd be damned if I was swimming naked again. Not after what just happened.

"He can't lie, but he didn't say he saw the body of the Oracle. He said the horns blew for his passing and they await a new one. Galwick controls when the horns blow in the Summer Court." He paused. "We didn't hear the horns here."

No. There had been no horns. Unless we missed them. But the horns were magical. We'd hear them throughout the Winter Court if they blew.

Rune cursed. "Why didn't I think of that? Stupid. All the court lords would have felt his passing and then ordered the horns."

"But Vespa...he said she burned at the stake."

Rune's face went serious as he nodded.

"He can't lie, so that means — she's really gone."

"I'm afraid so."

I couldn't handle the sorrow reflected in his eyes, so I barreled on. "But wouldn't the potions work better on her, on someone with the ability to lie?"

Rune shrugged. "Galwick may have seen it as an opportunity to get rid of her. He had the Oracle. If he had to wait a few days to get one of them to talk, I can see where he kept the Oracle instead of a witch."

The way he said it made me recoil. *Instead of a witch.* Of course, a fae life meant more to him. I hardened myself and nodded. "Then to the Spring Court it is."

SEVEN

Things were awkward. The damned pool. We'd agreed that it was best to leave the cave, sift from outside it. Though the chance anyone would track the sift was low, he didn't want to risk it. Considering we'd already had to use this cave in an emergency, I didn't think his concern was unwarranted.

Rune had already stripped bare and rifted his clothes away while I tried valiantly, yet failed, to not ogle him. He kept his back to me, standing at the water's edge. The cave itself was at least only chilled compared to what it could have been without my magic occasionally heating it up.

I stripped down to my underthings, dropped the pile by his feet and jumped in. I'd have magic this time to dry us off after, so he could get as naked as he wanted. I, on the other hand, had to keep some sort of reasonable head.

Underwater, I heard the rumble as he dove in behind me. On the other side, we wasted no time in getting out. A dusky sky greeted us along with a frigid breeze that instantly froze the water droplets to our skin. I immediately channeled the fire from the coals in the cave, weaving it around myself before turning my attention on him. Dry clothes on wet skin in this cold would only do so much good.

He hissed as my magic touched him. Earlier, we had discussed me using my witchery instead of him so he could conserve enough to sift us twice. It was practical, and this was a clinical type thing. So I'd easily agreed.

But why had I not considered how intimate this was before I started? I had begun at his shoulders, working my way down, and now I was left with a choice of continuing or not helping him.

His eyes shuttered as I made my choice to move on. I couldn't leave him there shivering, water droplets freezing to his skin. The sky darkened, the sun hiding behind a rose-colored cloud. We had slept the day away, and the temperature had nowhere to go but down. But I could be efficient, practical about it. No nonsense. Like a life witch healing someone.

Rune groaned as I moved closer to his hips, wrapping my magic around him and averting my eyes. Then, through clenched teeth, he grated out. "Move on to my legs, for Wall's sake."

I did as requested before dropping my magic and pulling on the clothes he'd rifted back into existence.

Once ready, Rune grabbed my hand, sifting us to the Spring Court and then again, bringing us closer to his friend's place using the same methods he used the other day.

Luckily for us, the Spring Court cave was a few hours' walk from his friends. He would need more rest to be prepared and for his to source to fully rejuvenate. If our combined magic always signaled where we were, then only his power fully back was acceptable. I sighed. That would mean at least a day in close proximity before we could get on with our task. But I couldn't deny that he was right. To do anything less would be folly.

The warm air of the Spring Court greeted us, a floral scent on the breeze and the sky, turning an oil painter's blend of pinks and purples. It took a minute or two for the numbness from that lake and the Winter Court to thaw, but how luscious it felt when it did. No one could deny the Winter Court held a peaceful beauty. If it wasn't for the cold, I'd have liked to visit it more. It just wasn't something this Summer Court witch could handle for long periods, and it wasn't as if Galwick allowed his witches to visit the other courts often.

Before us stood a small house in what was the trunk of a huge tree. Round windows glowed with an inner light, and as I looked closer between all the bark and moss, a staircase wrapped around the outside of the trunk.

The door at the bottom opened, and a fae man with red hair that grayed at the temples walked out with a basket. He whistled as he headed toward a small garden off to the side before he noticed us and came to a jarring halt.

I braced myself for anything.

"Rune!" the man yelped as he dropped the basket.

Rune loped up to him with a grin I'd never seen on his face. It was nearly boyish in its joy. They hugged in that way men do, slapping each other on the back, joining hands between their chests.

"Muriel! Get down here," Rune's friend called out over his shoulder.

A woman appeared at the top of the staircase, and I sucked in a breath. Instantly, I knew she was a witch. Fae knew us by scent, but among witches it was just a sense, a knowing, a kinship.

Who were these people? Fae and witch didn't just live together. And how did they know Rune?

Rune looked back toward me, that grin still on his face, stalling my heart. I'd rarely seen him crack anything more than a smirk. He looked...happy. And Goddess help me if I didn't light up right back at him with a grin of my own.

It was then that the fae man noticed me. His face lost some of its joy. In its place now was hesitancy, suspicion. But he covered it quickly with a small smile and then a twinkle in his eye. "Who do we have here? Did you finally bring someone home to us?" He elbowed Rune in the ribs, chuckling. Rune ducked his head with what might actually have been a bit of pink on his cheeks.

I swallowed. This...this was not what I had expected. Cut-throat killers? Someone who knew how to use every Faerie poison in the most efficient way? Yes. But a home? Were these his parents? Galwick was his father.

The confusion must have shown on my face as Rune introduced us. "Lily, this is my old tutor, Fenwyn, and his wife, Muriel. He was more of a father to me than, well—" Rune scratched the back of his head as he cast his gaze up to Muriel, who made her way down.

But I didn't need to hear more. Galwick seemed incapable of being a father figure to anyone. I moved forward and extended my hand to Fenwyn. "Pleased to meet you," I said as my eyes drifted up to Muriel.

Fenwyn returned my shake as a wide smile broke across his features. "Lily, is it?" he asked with a side-glance to Rune, which I didn't know how to interpret.

Muriel was slender with dark skin and long, braided hair. She rushed to Rune, and he picked her up and swung her around as they laughed. "So good to see you, my boy," she said.

He placed her back on the ground, and she lifted a hand to his cheek. "What are you doing here? Just yesterday Fenwyn went to town and heard some to-do about Galwick's men in the outskirts. Lord Sprayvale is likely in fits."

Rune's smile dropped. "Perhaps we should go, then. I don't want to bring trouble to your doorstep."

"What?" Fenwyn asked, dropping the basket to the stump of a small tree. "Galwick's men have something to do with you?"

I stood off to the side, an outsider to this seemingly found family.

Rune drove his hand through his hair, making the dark locks gleam in the sunlight. "Unfortunately, yes. I don't want to say too much. We've —" and then he looked at me as he motioned between us "— been given an assignment."

"By Galwick?" Fenwyn's face turned red, and he fisted his hand. "That man just won't stop trying to break you, will he?"

"Not Galwick. The Oracle, and the Matriarch..." Again, his eyes met mine, and Fenwyn and Muriel turned as well.

Muriel's eyes widened before she gave me a slight nod as Fenwyn leaned in and whispered my name to her.

"Perhaps we should talk inside," Rune said.

Muriel's smile slid away. The once joyous homecoming having now turned serious. "Of course." She moved to the door just behind her and held it open. "You're both welcome here."

Inside, a magical breeze circulated air about the room. You wouldn't have known you were inside a tree trunk. Everything felt light and breezy with the hint of honeysuckle in the air.

Muriel brought a tray of fruit, bread, and wine from the kitchen, while Fenwyn ushered us to sit down on the fluffy couches. Plants and colors decorated the room. A woven ottoman sat in the middle of the three couches with a brightly knit throw blanket on top. Muriel placed the tray down on top of it before serving the wine and handing it to us.

I hesitated. There was more than one kind of wine in the Summer Court, but I knew they could be enchanted while brewed.

"It's just winterberry wine. No effects." She smiled at me as she drank from her glass.

"Thank you," I murmured. I watched her with curious eyes as she sat down next to Fenwyn. She curled her feet up and leaned into his side. His arm came down around her, stroking her skin. I tried not to gape.

Fae and witch. I thought that was treason, but here they were. But then...Muriel. I'd heard that name when I was younger. A witch exiled. She was both in our coven and outside of it. One can never quite leave, but one can be made to not feel a part of. Sometimes that could be worse.

"So, what is this that you were saying about the Oracle?" Fenwyn asked as he leaned forward to grab some fruit and handing a portion of it to Muriel.

Rune told him that the Oracle and the Matriarch had given us an assignment, but he left out all the pertinent details. They seemed to understand that details were what got people into trouble.

When we asked about the horns for the Oracle, they told us no horns were blown in the Spring Court.

Muriel squeezed her eyes shut for a moment before she said, "The Matriarch has passed." Then she cast her gaze upon me. "Why did you not think to contact your sisters?"

"I was ordered not to allow myself access to them. And now…" I spread my hands wide. And while that instruction had set this mission vastly apart from others, it now sent a shiver down my spine that Muriel had contacted someone. Someone who could then tell Galwick where we were. A fear gripped me. Fear for Rune more so than myself.

"Who did you speak with?" My voice shook as I tried to push aside the realization that I worried for Rune's wellbeing.

His head shot up, honing in on my alarm. "Lily, what's the matter?"

"She just announced our presence here."

Muriel placed her wineglass down, an admonishing look on her face. "I did no such thing. Besides, I only speak to those I would trust with my life, with Fenwyn's." She threw me a pointed look, like she knew exactly the fear that had triggered me. "They keep it hidden that I live here with my mate. To do anything to harm *you* would harm us." Muriel's dark eyes lit with ire as she reached for Fenwyn's hand.

I swallowed down my anxiety, inclining my head to her. She was a witch married to a fae, and not just married. Mates. How? It must be incredibly rare.

I cleared my throat before speaking. "You have your allies among our sisters, I see. Does Lord Sprayvale know you are here?" I asked.

Fenwyn's eyes went from serious to mischievous. Leaning

forward, rubbing his hands, he said, "I've been working on something. I've created wards to glamour and hide this location. Rune knew our location. He sifts within the wards. But if you go outside of them, this just looks like a large tree. Nothing of interest. We've now setup a few places like this in all the courts, but the Summer." He stood, grinning like a child, before heading over to a desk that held all sorts of instruments and journals. Herbs and potions. Candles and crystals.

Rune mimicked the look, his eyes alight. It was like I saw an entirely different fae. Like so much of him had been hidden in the Summer Court, and here he felt free to be himself. Warmth filled my belly.

His gaze snagged mine as he caught me staring. My cheeks burned, and I looked away to where Fenwyn rummaged before picking something up and trotting back over with a spring in his step. Then he plunked a turquoise pebble into Rune's open hand.

"I've been experimenting with those same wards. Trying to make a portable one — for emergencies. So far, we've remained unnoticed."

Muriel made a choked noise.

Fenwyn cringed. "We've had a close call or two. But we've always been able to sift to one of our other places. But that's why I've been working on these portable ones. If somehow they come through the first line of wards, then this could save us or buy us time to get our things and sift."

Rune looked about the room. The place was cozy, and they clearly had their Cirrelean delights and comforts. "What about all this? Don't you worry something will be left behind that tells them where you went to."

"It's just stuff. Stuff we like, even love. But if we'd be distraught over its loss, we keep it in my Rift. And Muriel," he glanced to his wife, who stiffened, "has her own way of hiding things."

I studied the woman. She leaned forward, picked up her wine glass, and drank from it as she studied me back. Interesting. How would a witch be able to hide things? Unless she had some void powers. But there were no void witches anymore. That's what the coven claimed.

The coven...and she was no longer part of them. Not in any kind of way that meant much.

Fenywyn rubbed his hands together again. "Keep that pebble. Sounds like you two could find a need for it."

"Don't you need it? I can't take this from you if it means risking where you live," Rune said, extending it back to Fenwyn.

Fenwyn waved him off as he leaned back into the couch. "I have several, and none of them do yet what I want them to do. But if you have need to be hidden...if those shadows aren't doing the trick, then either of you can channel a tiny amount of your magic into the pebble. The radius on it is small, but enough to hide you both if you stand together. And it will only last a few minutes."

Rune slipped the rock into his pocket, making sure I noted where he put it. He gave it a little pat.

Fenwyn continued, "I think there is potential for those pebbles to conceal a larger area, last longer and potentially only need a bit of my or Muriel's magic every few days to charge them. I've been experimenting with chaining them together."

Rune and Fenwyn kept on discussing ideas about these pebbles. Turned out Rune liked to tinker. He'd even pulled a small journal from his Rift and was taking notes. They were like two mad apothecaries, carrying on about their latest discoveries or mishaps. Fenwyn even brought over a stack of notes, pointing out details that Rune should make note of.

It was...cute.

I didn't notice how much I was smiling until Muriel leaned forward. "So, we finally get to meet the Lethal Lily."

"Come again?" I asked, not even slightly sure what she meant.

"Rune calls you that."

I nearly choked on my wine, a bit of it dribbling down my chin. "He's spoken about me before?"

Muriel stood, beckoning me with a jerk of her head. "Come, you must have a lot of questions. It's late," she said with a glance at the windows, which now no longer glowed with the hues of sunset. "You probably also want to clean up. I gather you left without much notice."

I nodded along, but in my head, I still thought *Rune has spoken about me before?* Whatever did that mean? Why? Why would he have spoken of me to these two?

Muriel led me up the stairs, a slim hallway led around the trunk. It would be awash with light in the daytime but now was dark with a dry, cool breeze blowing through. Rooms sat to the inside.

She opened a door and led me in. The room was wedge-shaped. A bed with many pillows and blankets lay on the floor. It was homey. Above, a magical skylight showed a starry sky. Every now and again leaves danced into view, blocking out some of the stars.

"You'll be in here tonight," she said before opening another door. "Bathroom to wash up. We all use it, so be mindful to knock."

I nodded, but I couldn't help but wonder if Rune would sleep here too. He'd told the story of how we were partnered for this assignment.

Muriel rummaged about, looking for things. She came back with a towel and a bar of soap sat on top. "For you." She held them out, then leaned against the doorjamb to the bathroom. "Can I see it?"

I cocked my head before she reached out for my arm. "The tattoo. Do you mind?"

"Go ahead," I said as she turned my wrist to see the black markings of a dagger surrounded by lilies.

"Rune has the same one?" She looked up as she spoke.

I nodded, swallowing, not sure why this conversation was putting me on edge.

"This binds you two, you know."

"I do. Vespa said it would."

Muriel eyed me again, searching before she let out a small "hmmm," and released my arm.

I cleared my throat. "So you married a fae and said you were mates. I thought marriage between the two was impossible."

She smiled and looked up at the skylight. "Not impossible. Not accepted. Frowned upon. Illegal. Those are all better terms. No one can truly stop who you marry, and he is my fated mate. On some levels, a marriage was never necessary anyway."

My heart stilled before it began again at a rapid pace. "But mates between witch and fae..."

Muriel smiled. "It is exceedingly rare. They like for you to not know that. I'm surprised Vespa didn't mention it, especially to you."

"Why especially to me?" I held my breath.

Muriel's eyes crinkled at the corners. "You were her mentee, were you not?"

"One of a few. Yes." I chewed a lip. "Perhaps she didn't think I was ready."

Muriel studied me again, her dark eyes bouncing back and forth as she gauged me. Was she somehow reading me? "Perhaps," she said finally. "I'll let you wash up." She pushed away from the door and headed for the hall.

"Wait." I grabbed her arm with barely thinking. She turned, a question in her eyes. "Why does he call me lethal?"

Muriel smiled softly, her dark hair lit by the light behind her. "I think that is not my story to tell."

"But..." I stammered. "Why did he speak of me to you? He barely knew I existed."

Muriel took a step back toward me, reached a hand up, pushing my hair behind my ear. "Believe me. He knew you existed," she whispered before she turned and left.

I BATHED. MURIEL USED HER WITCHERY TO SPEED UP CLEANING AND DRYING my clothes. Halfway through my bath, she had knocked and placed them on a stool, leaving the door cracked open.

Now I stood in that same towel, drying my hair. Through the slightly ajar door, I could see Rune in the bedroom. He made it look tiny. His hair nearly brushed the ceiling.

Our eyes met and his dropped to my feet and back up again. They filled with heat while molten lava flowed through me. He'd seen me naked, multiple times, but this somehow felt even more intimate.

"I showed Lily to your room. We'll have dinner shortly." Muriel was speaking to him, and I paused drying my hair.

"Can I grab a pillow and blanket from here?" Rune's deep voice was easier to hear.

"Whatever for?" Muriel asked as a pit formed in my stomach as Rune stepped out of my view.

"I'll take the couch." He paused. I could practically visualize him rubbing the back of his neck. "Just less complicated that way." His heavy steps sounded out.

"I see. She doesn't..." Muriel's voice trailed off like a question.

A door was pulled tight before their footsteps retreated.

I placed the peach-colored fluffy towel down and stared at myself in the mirror. The molten hot pit that had formed in my stomach moments ago now felt like nausea.

"Get a grip," I said to my reflection, but my brown eyes were wide with fright. This attraction. It was a losing battle.

Today I'd seen sides of him I'd never imagined seeing. And if I admitted hearing him arrange to sleep somewhere else bothered me, then I was a hypocrite. But it was getting harder and harder to hate him.

My hands trembled as I used some of Muriel's lotions on my face. "So the incredibly hot but murdery fae man makes your insides go mushy. We can deal with this," I spoke to myself in the mirror, "I have a job to do. He made the right choice with sleeping on the couch. Once our job is done, we can go our separate ways. Because I can *not* act on this attraction."

I set the lotion bottle down on a counter with a clack as I breathed in deeply. I had no idea what going our separate ways would entail. We've committed high treason. I could potentially seek refuge in witch clans within other courts. With what we'd done, I had to have broken some ancient agreement between witches and the Summer lords. But Rune? He would be enemy number one in all the other courts. And damn this feeling that meant I cared what happened to him after.

CHAPTER
EIGHT

We stayed two nights and left early the next morning. It was best that way. If Galwick had any idea where we were going, then we had to proceed with caution. We spent the early hours stealthily moving through the forest. The Spring Court abounded with meadows and gurgling brooks. We always took the long way around, sticking to the trees.

Twice, Rune pressed me against a tree, wrapping his shadows around us. I both loathed and loved it.

Finally, we crested a hill, and there, not far below us, was the cave. A cliff-side of white and gold brown rock. The cave was nestled within the saddle of these rolling hills, but the cliffs thrust upward awkwardly in the middle, like some god or fate had spliced them, blunting their smooth edge. Near the cliff was a worn path. We'd been following it to this very point.

The cave's mouth opening was larger than the one in the Winter Court. It would take more magic for us to conceal it. More time, which meant we'd be attracting whatever fae beasts were out there for longer. But this was the mission.

I was about to head down into the saddle when Rune's hand shot out, holding me back. He crouched, and I followed his lead. His fae senses likely picked up on something my human ones hadn't.

"Shit," he murmured before he frantically looked about before dragging me over to an area where the rocks created a small overhang.

I'd gathered he wanted us to hide there, but I didn't see how we'd fit.

"Lay down," he hissed.

I quickly lay on my back and scooted in with zero thought about what his plan was. Next thing I knew, he crawled across me, pressing his body on top of mine.

"If you have any ability in water magic to glamour us, do it now. If I use my shadows, the Wild Hunt might sense it."

I froze at his mention of the Wild Hunt — an army of the undead led by the Huntsman that stopped at nothing but the death of its current mission. And the Huntsman liked to offer his services to the highest bidder, which recently had been Galwick.

Water magic? I shook my head. "It doesn't work the same way as fae."

"Then let's hope they are looking for a shadow magic wielder." Water appeared and quickly glided around to encapsulate us. I watched, dumbstruck, as he created a glamour that looked like the rocks we hid in, but from our side, we could see movement on the other.

He shouldn't be adept at this. He was a shadow wielder.

"Your pulse is pounding. Breathe. They'll sense it," Rune said. "My glamour will only dampen our sounds."

But my pulse wasn't pounding from only the Wild Hunt's presence. He was something he shouldn't be. A dual-wielder, and he'd kept it hidden from everyone, which made me wonder what else he hid.

The sounds of the Hunt now reached my human ears. Dozens, if not hundreds, of feet ground in the rocky dirt. Metal clanked. The breeze brought the stench of decay, their rotting flesh.

I could barely make out Rune's eyes in the dark he'd created with his glamour. He stared straight at me as he adjusted his arms so his fingers could smooth over my brows. He breathed in deep, his belly pushing into mine. It steadied me. I synced my breath to his as his fingers moved into my hair, massaging my scalp. I wanted to purr, but knew any sound now could spell disaster.

Footsteps shuffled right by us. Occasionally, a bit of pebble even got thrown into our nook. Any one of those fae beasts might notice the rolling rock didn't stop where it should. We held our breath, not wanting to make a sound. Instead of watching the feet go by mere inches from our heads, as the dead growled and rasped, we stared at each other, grounding one another.

Time drew out as more and more shuffled by, a few even crawled by as they no longer had legs. Those had my fingers curling into Rune's leathers, but the undead army didn't seem to be on the hunt for us or for anyone at the moment.

Eventually, the last of the Hunt passed by, but we continued to lie there. My fingers trembled, and I realized at some point I had curled them around Rune's waist. His leathers had come up, exposing his skin, which was where my fingers now lay. I knew I shouldn't. It would only lead to temptation, but I couldn't stop myself after witnessing all his tawny skin in the Winter Court. I stroked lightly. Goosebumps trailed in their wake, his skin warm and soft under my touch. His eyes shuttered as he dropped his head.

My core went molten with him on top of me like this. I adjusted my leg, so I cradled him more. When he tilted his head back up, his forehead grazed along my cheek, and I shivered at the touch of our skin.

Tell me you want this.

That's what he said the other morning. And Goddess help me, I wanted it even though my brain kept telling me not to.

He moved his hand so his thumb rested below my chin while his fingers splayed along my cheek. He put a tiny bit of pressure to tilt my chin up.

"Lily," he whispered.

His eyes drifted to my mouth, and I wanted to feel his kiss. When my tongue shot out and wet my lips, his arousal throbbed between us and my breath hitched.

His thumb brushed over my bottom lip, pulling it down ever so slightly. I arched my back, pushing my breasts into his chest.

I so needed an answer to the question plaguing me. "What is this—"

Armored feet came inches away from us, cutting my words off. We both froze as boot-clad toes faced us. I tried to calm my now racing heart. Did they sense us?

A rattling groan and then the sound of water splashing on rock. Not water, urine. And urine meant this was not the undead. No, it was the Huntsman himself, taking a leak on the rock right above our heads.

Rune held himself rigid above me.

My heart hammered wildly.

The stream of urine splashed loudly and then stopped. His feet ground in the dirt as the Huntsman took a step back as he adjusted himself. I closed my eyes, hoping this wasn't my last few seconds of life with my hair potentially soaked in the piss of the Huntsman.

He backed up again and paused. We held our breath, and judging on how tightly Rune now held himself, he was ready to unleash his shadows like the garrote shadow he'd used on that foot soldier. Neither of us dared speak. The horde of undead couldn't be that far gone. The Huntsman could easily call them back.

I reached out and found embers in the cave nearby. They must have camped there. It wasn't much, but it was enough for me to weave fire far behind him.

The Huntsman's feet ground again, his knees coming into view. He was bending down to look. The urine likely giving away Rune's glamour as it travelled beneath what looked like solid rock.

The rasp of a sword coming out of its sheath rang out.

My instincts took over, and I released the weave. An explosion of fire boomed far off in the distance.

The Huntsman stood, feet shuffling as he turned before he took off at a run in the direction of my fire decoy. The snarls of the undead started once more as he called his army to him to investigate.

"Can you do it again, but throw it further? Draw them away even more?" Rune whispered.

I nodded. "I need to see to aim better."

He stilled for a moment, likely reaching out with his senses before he nodded and began to inch himself off me.

I missed the weight of him, but now was no time for any of that. We crawled out of the overhang. Rune held his fingers to his lips.

I rolled my eyes at him before I cast my gaze to the horizon. A thin tendril of smoke rose in the distance. I'd hit some trees with my last one.

I channeled again, harnessing from those smoking trees. Earlier, we'd passed a small lake surrounded by a rocky shore. We'd skirted around it as Galwick's men lounged about. I hoped they were still there or nearby because an idea brewed in my head.

I wove fire again, but this time I knew exactly where I wanted to send it. Except... I hesitated.

"What's wrong?" Rune asked.

"I have an idea. One that could distract two problems on our tails. But I can't see far enough."

"Shouldn't the general area be good enough?"

I hummed. "I want to hit the rocks by that lake we passed earlier."

Rune grinned as he grasped what I aimed to do.

I nodded, continuing, "It'll get everyone's attention. But I just can't see well enough."

"Let me try this." Rune moved behind me and grasped my shoulders. Heat radiated off him as he took a step closer before sending his magic through me.

My senses sharpened. The crashing of the Wild Hunt through the forest toward the trees I burned was a cacophony to my ears, and the lake we passed was a blue shining gem in the distance. I could make out the rocky shore, see the large boulder near where Galwick's men had loafed about and the mud on their boots. They were busy packing, getting their armor on. They must have heard the explosion, too. But they'd be too slow. I grinned as I let my second fire weave wrap around the boulder before I gently tapped it to explode.

With my heightened sense of hearing, the crack pierced my ears, leaving a ringing behind, but I remained focused as the boulder split in two. Galwick's men dropped to their knees as rock shrapnel pelted them. Then everything there turned to mayhem.

Rune stepped back, and my normal hearing and sight returned. All that was left in my vision was a blue puddle far out with smoke rising over it.

"Well done," he murmured. "Now, to get our job done."

"How did you?" I stood there, stunned. He'd given me fae sight and hearing. "How did you know to do that?"

A broad smile broke across his face. "Fenwyn and Muriel."

We got to work quickly, setting the box in the cave and hiding it. Then it was time to disguise the cave opening. We moved right to the outside of the cave after a quick look to be sure the Wild Hunt hadn't returned. It seemed the explosion had caused a nice ruckus for Galwick's men.

Outside the cave, nerves flickered all over my body. The attraction between us was becoming a palpable thing. But did it matter if I found him attractive? If he'd killed so many of my sisters and brothers, could I even consider it?

"What is it?" he murmured as he took my hand and placed his other on the cool rock of the high cliffs.

"What do you mean?"

"Something flickered in your eyes there for a second. Something not pleasant." His thumb grazed along my hand.

I glanced away. I should ask him. I should put it out there. If he admitted it, then that would help me control these urges. So I straightened my spine. "How many witches did Galwick order you to murder?"

His hand slid from mine as he stepped back. My stomach sank even though I had known the answer. The look in his eyes could only mean one thing. And my reaction pissed me off. How could I want this? How could knowing the truth make me feel so unbelievably sad? So broken-hearted? I leaned into the anger.

"How many? Tell me."

"One," he whispered as he met my glare. "I refused after that. I refused to be a part of an extermination once I figured out what his plans were."

"You expect me to believe that?" I'd expected a number, but him lying about it was even worse. But fae can't lie, and a tiny amount of hope flittered into my heart.

"I swear to you. I refused after Braidoc."

I flinched at the name. Braidoc had been in lessons with me since we were children. We'd been friends. He'd been the first person I slept with.

Rune's eyes were huge, pleading. "It was you. You, when they cremated his body convinced me to never raise my dagger to another witch."

I huffed in disbelief. "You weren't even at Braidoc's death rites."

"I was. I hid. In my shadows. And it was your crying." Rune reached out to my hands, giving them a squeeze. "The utter pain I saw in your eyes nearly devastated me. I caused it—" His voice broke.

Tears welled in my eyes. "He was a friend."

Rune hung his head. "I know. I knew then too, and I hated myself for it. I've hated myself every day since, every time I look at you, and then I hate myself more because I can't stop looking at you." His fingers rubbed over the backs of my hands.

But it was too much. I pulled them away and dashed away the tears. His words set something tumbling inside me, but now was not the time. At least hearing him admit it doused the attraction I felt. "Let's just get this job done."

Rune's mouth worked like he wanted to say more. Slowly he nodded, took my hand, and we closed our eyes. Joining our magic now was easy, but I hadn't prepared for the emotions that came with it. Instead of the usual dance of our magic, we were both tentative creatures, reaching out to one another. Scared to be hurt. But when we finally met, it was like a big hug. Sorrow filled me. Guilt. And a thought: *She'll never see me like I see her.* I focused my senses on the job at hand. Best to get the job done lest we attract unwanteds.

We focused our intentions, conceal the cave, make it impenetrable for a time.

By the time it was done, my tears had dried, but my heart was heavy with sorrow. For Braidoc. For Rune who had followed orders. He said he refused after it, but witches kept dying. That was also when Rune began visiting the other courts.

Without a word, he neared, pulled me close and sifted us.

CHAPTER
NINE

The Autumn Court greeted us. Out of the all the beauty of each court, this one was my favorite.

We'd spoken about this earlier as we'd headed to the cave. We'd place the scroll in the Spring cave followed by sifting to the Autumn Court, where we'd rest to be sure we were in top form by the following day.

Reds, oranges, and yellows abounded. A cool breeze carried leaves on it, letting them slowly drift around us. It wasn't happening right now, but I bet when we woke in the morning, our breath would fog.

I breathed in deeply. The apple-scented air was energizing and a needed change of pace after our discussion.

"We should find somewhere to rest." Rune walked in front of me, his shoulders slightly slumped.

I followed, hating that I caused that, hating that I hated it too. My emotions were in a tangle.

Eventually, a small hut came into view. One that had seen better days. Rotting planks of wood with moss wedged between them jutted up from the ground amongst tightly growing trees. Small paned windows sat on either side of the door. Outside, a short, decrepit fence that lay mostly broken on the ground encircled the area in front of the hut.

"We're a few hours' walk to the cave. We're likely far enough out of their searching bounds, but we should lie low. No fire." He barely met my eyes as he stepped over an area of broken fencing.

So, an entire afternoon of lying low. Together. Alone.

He opened the door to a dusty interior before rifting into existence the small bag of provisions Fenwyn and Muriel had sent us off with. He plunked it down on the table in the middle of the room as if to say *food here if you want it.* Off to the side was a ratty mattress, and on the other, an armchair near the fireplace.

He stood in front of a window, rubbing the back of his neck and studiously not looking my way. "I'm gonna have a nap." He laid down on the mattress and rolled toward the wall.

Which left me standing there until I moved over to the armchair and sat down with nothing to do except stare at his back and think. I opened the sack of food, pulled out a few dried goods, and ate them.

Memories of Braidoc rose to the surface. We had slept together a few days before my first Spring Equinox, the celebration where fae males could sleep with whatever maidens they chose. I'd asked him one night when we'd been drinking. The idea of sleeping with some fae for the first time during that blasted celebration infuriated me. He'd obliged, but it'd only made the tensions in our friendship even more because of his developing feelings for me. I'd known it yet still asked. My own selfishness had won out. It turned everything into a mess. He wanted more. I wanted to just be friends.

When he died of a single stab wound to the heart, I grieved him as well as the friendship I'd ruined and would never get to atone for. I'd never get to apologize.

And I'd never get rid of the feeling that maybe if he'd been with me the night he died, then maybe he would still be alive. It was a small comfort when the life witch who found him said, "Whoever stabbed him had surgical precision."

Braidoc had passed quickly. But the witches since then?

I stifled a yawn as my heavy eyes drifted to the steady rise and fall of Rune's chest. The witches murdered after Braidoc had been mutilated: marks on their wrists, ankles and neck from being tied down with something. Then it was death by a thousand cuts. Fingers missing. Disembowelled. Whoever killed them had enjoyed it.

I stared at Rune's back. Precision killer for one and the others were deaths by someone who got off on it.

The killers weren't the same.

A HAND COVERED MY MOUTH.

I jerked awake. Rune stood in front of me, his breath white and panting, a finger to his lips.

Outside, the light of day was gone. The cold set into my bones like a ghost wafted straight through me. Everything was murky and wavery, unreal.

The door to the hut creaked open, and there was Vespa. My breath stalled in my chest. She was dead...supposedly, but my heart leapt at seeing her whole and healthy.

Rune swiveled and lifted a dagger, pointing it at her. "Get back!" His other hand went to cross in front of me.

I pushed him away, trying to stand, but the world around me swam, and I staggered back into the seat. "Are you mad?"

His eyes were enormous, the pupils blown, as he glanced at me as if I was the one ranting.

Vespa paused, dressed in one of her everyday dresses. She always favored them over pants and shirts. She, one time, jokingly told me it was her aesthetic. "No one would follow a Matriarch running around in fighting gear." She'd then eyed me up and down, making her point.

At the time, I'd resolved that if I somehow became Matriarch one day, then it wouldn't matter what I wore.

I made it to my feet and pushed against Rune's arm to go to Vespa, whose face was solemn, sorrowful.

He pushed me back. "What are you doing? Don't go to it!"

"It? It's Vespa!" I pushed again, this time taking him by surprise with my strength as he staggered forward. I'd use my fire magic if I had to.

Vespa stood outside the door. "Come, Lily. There is so much we must discuss." She beckoned for me, so I took a step forward, wanting to go to her. She had the answers, but Rune grabbed my hand and tugged me back to him.

"That is not Vespa," he hissed and gave me a shake. The world around me went fuzzy and swoopy, like I'd had one too many drinks.

My head began to ache. "What did you put in the food?"

"He drugged you, my dear. Come outside. We must talk. I shouldn't have told you to trust him," Vespa said.

Rune grabbed me with both hands, having relinquished the dagger to the seat behind me. "Get behind me! I have to kill it."

I pulled away from him as my heart beat wildly. I shouldn't trust him? She'd told me to trust him. And I was just getting used to the idea of trusting him.

Nausea churned in my gut as I tugged away. Rune's grip on me slipped, and I fell to the floor with a thud, banging my hip on the chair.

"Don't get closer to it, Lily." Rune's voice was full of fear. *For me.* His face crumpled in a grimace before he gripped his head and screamed, "Get out of my head, bitch!"

I scooted back. Away from him, away from Vespa.

Vespa watched me, shaking her head like she did whenever we had disappointed her. "Dear, you must come to me. He's obsessed with you. He'd do anything to keep you. You must come with me. I'll get you out of here."

My body trembled while black oily sludge coated all my

thoughts. It made it hard to think, to do anything. I was crawling towards her without thinking it, without wanting it.

No! The sludge was oozing into my mind, taking control. I pushed at it. But the oil remained. Something was wrong. Vespa was *wrong*. And that belief buoyed my strength to stop crawling towards her. So I focused, grew my intent and pushed at the blackness covering my mind. Vespa's body jerked, but only momentarily. The ooze, though, had cleared back to a haze.

"Now! Lily. I won't say it again." Her voice was like when I was a child disobeying her, and I wanted to please her.

Rune fell to his knees. "No. She can't hate me. She's my mate."

Rune's words stopped my heart. *Mate.* But I had no time to dwell on that. He wasn't looking at me, trapped by whatever this version of Vespa did to him. I had to focus, to keep pushing at the haze, trying to banish it entirely from my mind. For him. For me.

Vespa flickered. Her clothes and image appearing and reappearing. But it revealed what was underneath: something dead.

My brain churned slow as molasses. Trying to name what I knew this creature was felt like walking through the bogs in the Summer Court. It took all my focus to keep the haze at bay, its attacks relentless. But then finally I had it: *sluagh*, a master at breaking down mental shields and manipulating you.

Rune groaned. Sweat dripped down his face as he held his dagger up, pointing it at himself, right at his throat.

Vespa crooned, "He's distracted. Kill him now and be done with it. I'll finish this mission with you. Just give me the journal, so I can see what the Oracle wrote."

My heart hammered. Every time she spoke, it was so real, so like her. But it wasn't. She wrote the journal, and likely with the Oracle's help. The sluagh only wanted me to think she was Vespa.

I had to end this and free Rune before he succumbed to her. "Rune," I screamed. "It's a sluagh. Whatever you're seeing isn't real."

But nothing changed. He was losing his own mental battle against her as the dagger inched closer to his Adam's apple.

He hadn't let us light a fire, so I reached for my dagger at my thigh. The sluagh was intent on Rune, her eyes alight with glee as the dagger he held began to dig in. Her attacks on me had lessened. Holding us both was too difficult. A tiny bead of blood welled on his throat, and as she caught the scent, her eyes shuttered in ecstasy.

Now! I flung my dagger at her while she was distracted, hitting her directly in the chest.

Rune gasped. Both he and his dagger dropped to the floor.

"Fire," I yelled, and he summoned a spark at the tips of his fingers as he came back to himself. I snatched it. Even the tiniest amount was all I needed. I wove it into a dagger of fire and threw it straight between her eyes.

The sluagh keeled over backwards with a sickening thud, the wound sizzling. Rune still breathed heavily as he stood, holding a hand to his throat. He clomped to the door, drawing his sword and slicing it down. The sluagh's head came free, and he kicked it away. With her glamour gone, her body was only a rotting corpse. The stench of her and the frying flesh made me gag. But Rune wasn't done. He grabbed her arm and dragged the body away and toward the edge of the woods by the hut.

Once back, he leaned against the doorjamb, looking utterly exhausted. Blood ran down his throat. It would heal soon enough. He wiped at it, flinging blood to the floor.

"Are you ok?" His voice was raspy.

I nodded, staring at where the sluagh's body had been. "She was so real." I hadn't even smelled her rotting flesh, and that was a scent I wouldn't forget for a long time.

"Yea," was all he said as he thumped into the room before collapsing on the chair I had fallen asleep in.

I stood to close the door he'd left open, but before I did I said, "Fire please."

Rune summoned it at his fingertips, and I gently threaded from it, wove it around the exterior of the house. Nothing could get too close without us knowing now. The fire trap would make noise and not blow us all up.

"I warded it."

Rune only nodded as he slumped forward and placed his head in his hands. I swallowed. He looked defeated.

"What did she show you?" It had to have been bad to shake him like this.

He shook his head, but the front of his leathers shone with his blood.

"You're still bleeding. How bad did you cut yourself?"

He leaned back, wiping at his neck again. His hand trembled as he took in his red-covered fingers. "Fuck. The Oracle warned me this could be a sign. We have to get those boxes placed." He flicked out a finger, creating a blaze in the fireplace that didn't consume the logs someone had once placed there. No smoke to give us away, but warmth quickly permeated the small room.

"Well, we're not going to complete the mission right this second. Here, let me help you." I grabbed for the small medicinal pouch I carried everywhere. I may not be a life witch, but all witches knew the basics. Fae did not. Why bother when you heal so quickly?

Except he wasn't healing quickly. What did that mean?

Without thinking, I dropped down in between his knees, and he sucked in a breath. "What are you doing?" He shifted back into the seat, creating space.

I tucked my chin as I opened the vial of salve. With a generous scoop on my fingers, I leaned forward to rub it onto his neck. On closer inspection, it was healing, just slowly.

He hissed as the ointment hit his skin. He wouldn't be used to the burn of it.

"The burn means it's working." I removed my finger from his skin, looking up to his face. His eyes were huge, and his hands gripped the arms of the chair. "Why aren't you healing more quickly? What did you mean it was one of the signs?"

"The Wall. It's...the Oracle said it's blocking our magic flowing into our world from the human lands. If it's happening to me, then I bet it's been happening to Galwick now for a while. He said the strongest would see it first."

"Then why wouldn't Galwick want us to complete this mission?" I sat back on my heels.

"Please get up," he groaned as he scrubbed his hand over his face.

And it was then I realized where I sat and why he'd sucked in a breath when I'd sat there to begin with. My cheeks burned. But I stayed where I was, letting the tension build. My core clenched as my body warmed. "I believe you, you know."

He peeked through his hand at me. "Wall, get up."

I wasn't going anywhere. "I believe you."

He sighed. "Believe me about what?"

"About Braidoc. The other witches."

He stilled. Only the wind creaking through the eaves of the hut made a sound as our shared look intensified.

"What did the sluagh show you?"

He didn't answer. Didn't move other than to avert his gaze as a pinkness grew on his cheeks, making my stomach swoop.

"What did the sluagh show you about your mate?" It wasn't until I said it that the jealousy tore through me. He had a mate. Did he know who she was? And why wasn't he with her?

Just when I thought he wouldn't speak, he said, "My mate staring at me with pure hatred. Scorn. Disgust." The light of the flames flickered in his eyes as he watched the fire.

I swallowed the lump in my throat. "Do you know her? Your mate."

He nodded, his gaze sliding back to me. There was something there in that look. Something stripped bare in him, raw, unfiltered, vulnerable. He wanted me to know, to understand, and the intensity of it made me clench my thighs together.

I glanced to the floor not knowing what to do with the utter flood of emotions that sank deep down into my belly. I wanted to get out of there. My limbs shook with it. I was torn between jealousy and hope.

Fenwyn and Muriel.

What was I doing? Playing with fire. He had a mate. And the only fae-witch mating I'd ever known had told me themselves how rare it was. This attraction between us had to end.

I pushed back, rocking up onto my feet. I stood and turned, but his hand whipped out and grabbed my wrist. His warmth encircled me, his touch electric. My heart lurched as he kept his head down, rubbing a thumb over my skin. "I've known who my mate is for a long time, but she's always looked at me with hatred."

"Why would she do that? She's your mate. Aren't mates instantly in love?" *But hadn't I always done that?*

The wind creaked through the hut. Leaves scattered across the floor, taking some of the warmth of the fire with it. I shivered.

"She has no idea," he whispered.

My heart thudded heavily, and my breath grew shorter.

"Why doesn't she know?" My voice was small, unsure. Nervous. Full of anticipation as I leaned in.

He looked up, his dark eyes holding depths that I'd never seen before. The vulnerability from before now laced with hope. "Because I haven't told her. And..." he trailed off as his grip on my wrist tightened. "Lily," he whispered with so much anguish as he pulled me toward him, placing his forehead against my stomach.

My chest was tight, like I might explode at any second. Some instinct guided me. I reached toward him with my magic, let it delve into his chest. He sucked in a breath, and I used my other hand to lift his chin. "And?" I wanted to hear it.

His gaze bore into me. "And she doesn't feel it. It's not as apparent to her because," he drew in a breath as I frowned. I knew fae women who'd identified their mate upon first sight. Not even — first being in a room with each other. And I'd never felt that.

His other hand came to my hip. "Because she's a witch."

His eyes implored me, and his fingers tightened into my leathers.

Because she's a witch.

It was like a polearm to my chest. I could barely breathe.

"It's you. It's always been you, since that first Spring Equinox you attended." He stifled a laugh. "Wall, I almost claimed you for that night. It was the equinox celebration after all, but I knew if I had you even once, then I'd never be able to stop."

My hand drifted to his shoulder, tightening into the straps there to hold whatever amounts of weapons he had, relishing his words but reeling from the shock that he claimed there was a mate bond between us.

"I used to watch you dance at all the parties and wished you were doing it just for me — remembering that one time we danced — but all the other men watched. I never drank because I couldn't bear to find myself with anyone other than you in the morning. I spent every day in the court looking for you wherever I went. Hoping to see you, dreading to see you because you'd see what a horrible creature I truly was, Then there was Braidoc. They were direct orders. I tried everything I could to get out of it, to convince Galwick it wasn't the way. But that made him want me to do it all the more. And then I saw — heard — what I'd done to you by obeying Galwick. And I hated myself. After that I refused, threatened to throw myself on the mercy of the Winter Court. Nearly lost my head for it, but I couldn't do that to you again. And now here we are."

I sucked in tiny breaths.

"Please say something."

But I didn't need to. At that moment, I knew the truth of his words. I'd seen his character over and over again on this assignment. Seen him, the true him, with his friends. Now I understood why, as much as I resisted, I always found myself drifting to him. Trying to find him at every event. And now that I knew what it was and who he really was, something clicked into place.

A desire tore through me that I never expected. I leant over and kissed him, clasping his cheeks between my hands. His lips were at first hesitant, before he kissed me back. But then he pulled away. "What are you doing?"

I shoved at his shoulders, pushing him back into the chair before I straddled his lap. "Having my way with you. What does it look like?"

I'd never released my magic, and now I fed more toward him, wrapping around his source. He groaned as I kissed along his neck. Where he'd cut himself was healing nicely. He flicked a finger and all the blood disappeared.

Mate.

It felt right. Wrapping around his magic like this was intoxicating, and when he unspooled some of his magic to dance with mine— ecstasy.

I kissed along the column of his throat until he ducked his chin to catch my mouth with his.

"Don't toy with me. Are you sure?" he asked as his hands dove into my hair and tugged me back so he could see me.

I nodded.

"I need to hear the words. Tell me you want this." He wrapped his arms around me and stood, hauling me up with him.

"I want this. I want you." And as shocked as I was to admit it, it was true. Was it the bond? I'd always found him attractive, and after getting to know him, I knew my attraction wasn't wrong. He really was loyal to Cirrelea. Loyal to me.

"Tell me one thing," I said, "why did the Oracle choose you?"

"The Fates told him the task needed fated mates. Fated witch and fae mates. Fenwyn and Muriel weren't an option. He said they had other purposes. And he always knew there was more than what Galwick had me doing. That I was meant for more. That everything Galwick would put me through would only train me for what was to come." He shook his head, making his hair fall into his eyes. "*Train* is the wrong word. Teach me what I needed to know, show me that what Galwick was trying to do was not the way." His fingers dug into my hips as we shared a moment.

"Hmmm," was all I said as I brushed the hair from his eyes. The longing between us threatened to snap like a bowstring.

Rune walked us over to the mattress on the floor. "Stand," he said.

I slid my feet down, kissing him as I did. Once I hit the ground, he pulled back, forcing me to lean in. But he only smiled and turned me around, pressing my back to his chest. "Any more questions?" His voice held a note of amusement.

"If I think of any—" A moan escaped me as he swept my hair to the side while he placed hot kisses along the back of my neck. His hands slid from my stomach to my back, where he began to unlace my corset strings on my leathers until I grew impatient and shrugged out of them myself. Behind me, I heard him doing the same until he pressed back against me. Bare skin to bare skin. The feel of his sparse spattering of chest hair along my back made me shiver and my nipples harden.

"Don't you want to see me?" I asked.

"Shh. I like the anticipation." His hand drifted across my collarbone to grab my chin and turn me for a kiss full of tongue, want and need, while his other hand gripped my hip bone.

He pulled back. "I'm sorry I followed orders with Braidoc. I need you to know that before we..." he whispered against my lips as he pressed his forehead to mine as his hand drifted over my abdomen, making my skin pebble with goosebumps.

I raised a hand, sliding it along his now unkempt beard. "I think I understand now. And I know you showed him mercy that another assassin wouldn't."

Rune stilled.

"What is it?" I was becoming near feral with need.

"Do you not know who the other assassin is?" The slow caressing of his hands stopped.

"Does it matter? It wasn't you." I nipped at his lips. "That's all that matters to me. If Braidoc was singled out by Galwick to die, then you showed him mercy. And..." I drew in a shaky breath as Rune's hand spread out over my throat. Not a threat, a claiming. "You may have had the sword, but Galwick is the true killer, a coward-killer having you do all his dirty work for him."

I tried to turn in Rune's arms, but his hand on my throat pinned me in place as he reclaimed my mouth with passion. He pressed against my back, the heat and feel of his skin luxurious. "You feel so good," he murmured as his other hand trailed toward where I was growing wet with need. My hips moved of their own accord, beckoning him. Every night since that morning, I'd wanted him there. And now his fingers circled, and I let out a throaty moan.

Rune throbbed against my back at the noises I made, and I couldn't take it anymore. I turned in his arms and this time, he let me, his fingers trailing around my throat.

Facing him, he brought both trembling hands up to cup my face before he kissed me, sweetly at first but quickly turning heated. I reveled in it, in the feel of his kiss, the smoothness of his skin, his taste, his scent. My hands trailed over his chest to his back and down to the firmness of his ass before sweeping them over his hips, causing his breath to hitch before I took him in my hands.

I pumped once, twice before he broke the kiss, "Ahh…you're lethal. Keep that up and this may be over before we've begun." He took my hand and led us to the mattress, guiding me to kneeling with him.

"Tell me when you knew I was your mate," I said as I trailed kisses down his neck, his chest.

"Again?" his arms pulled me up, before guiding me to lay back.

"Yes. I want to hear everything. Feel everything." I gripped him, flicking a thumb over the top. His hips rocked.

"It was one of Galwick's parties." His fingers slipped back between my folds, and I almost didn't care to hear more. "It was the Spring Equinox, four years ago. It must have been your first one."

I swallowed, remembering it. Remembering *him*. I had been so scared. The fae men drank the wine and then chose from the women, fae and human alike. It was my first party. I was newly eighteen and expected to attend. But I had been a virgin up until a few nights before. The last thing I had wanted was for some fae man to be my first. Braidoc and I had ruined our friendship, and on that night, I'd been hurting with the loss of my friend.

But before the drinking began, Rune actually danced. It was the first and only time I'd seen him do so. He wasn't yet known as the assassin, only Galwick's bastard son. And for that alone, I'd hated him.

But I danced with the other women at the bonfire until one played for partners. Rune and I wound up together.

"We danced." His smile along my cheek tickled as he nipped at my ear while his fingers danced at my core. "You were breathtaking, but when our hands met, a bolt went straight through me. It was then that I knew, without a doubt, what you were."

His fingers picked up their pace. My head fell back, and I moaned before getting out, "And what am I?" As I rode the tightening between my legs. Oh Wall, I was so close.

He sucked at where my neck met my shoulder. "My mate, my other half, my everything—" he moved to look me in the eye "— my love. Now come for me. I want to watch you unravel."

The world shattered around me as my orgasm hit. Wave after wave crested, and he helped me ride them all, covering my moans with his mouth.

As I came down, chest heaving, he kneeled between my legs, stroking himself as he watched me. It didn't matter that he'd just made me come the hardest I ever had in my entire life. My body already began to warm again as his eyes filled with want and need.

I moved to sit up. He no longer touched me. "Rune…" I breathed, but his shadows slinked out of him, wrapping around me, holding me gently in place.

"I'm memorizing every inch of you. I don't ever want to forget this moment. You. Spread before me like a feast, skin glowing and satisfied," he paused, his throat bobbing, "by me. I never thought this would ever happen. I thought that the only time I'd see you like this was in my dreams."

I breathed his name again, pulling at his shadows, which now only served to heighten my need for him. I wanted him, not his shadows. But he toyed with me, letting the shadows caress up my ribs, over my breasts, along my arms before circling around my wrists. And then he sent one devilish one between my legs, making me gasp and writhe.

"I could make you come again just like this. Would you like that?" His eyes were heated, his focus switching from between my legs to my face.

The shadows were just as deft as his fingers, helping me climb higher and higher. I bit my lip, eyeing his hands on himself. "I want those hands on me. I want *you*, not your shadows." I pulled against his dark restraints as my legs began to shake.

Finally he let himself go, so he could lean over me, letting me feel the tip of him at my entrance. "You could have both," he whispered before his mouth crashed against mine. His shadows expanded and slid along my legs, pushing my knees further apart. "Is this ok?" he asked.

I lifted my hips. I wanted all of him, and he was teasing. He chuckled as he pulled away just enough. I growled as his shadows kept up their rhythmic pace on my clit but always backing off when I got too close. It was frustratingly decadent.

"Tell me what you want, mate." He nipped at my ear, kissed down my neck as I panted and writhed restlessly, not being allowed to release.

"I want you, and your shadows." I panted. I wanted all of him.

"Mmmm." His eyes flared like he liked what I'd said. "Can you be a bit more specific?" His hands now coasted along my sides, over my breasts as he shifted to take each nipple into his mouth and worship each one.

"I want you inside of me." His shadows disappeared from my arms and wrists, freeing me to finally touch him. As soon as my hands glided over his skin, we shared a moan. But I didn't stop at his chest. I dove straight down, grabbing onto him and positioning him. And then I looked him in the eye. "I want you to fuck me."

He stilled and throbbed in my hand. "You know what that means for our bond?"

I raised my hips, feeling the tip of him enter me. "You're my mate and nothing could feel more right."

His eyes shuttered close before he pushed his hips to fully seat himself inside of me. His head dropped on a groan, and then he was moving, slowly at first, nearly pulling all the way out before pushing back in. It was torturous, it was luscious. My name was a whisper and a plea on his lips before we both lost control. His shadows wrapped around me, caressing everywhere. My fire magic delved out, letting me place warm kisses all over him.

And then I was spiraling out of control. Sparks bloomed behind my eyes, and a golden cord wrapped tight around me, connecting me to him. Then he was right there, following behind me, chanting my name. With my eyes still squeezed shut, I could see him at the other end of the golden cord. He yanked at it, pulling me close. His hands dove into my hair on either side of my face, before his lips found mine in a heated kiss that was both tender and feral.

"Mate," he whispered. "I've longed for you."

The cord between us pulled tight, and then an emotion flooded me as a tiny tingle spread over my wrist. One of pure adoration. Opening my eyes, Rune lay over me, one hand along the side of my face and his thumb tilting my chin. "I don't know about you, but I think I'd be up for that a few more times." He leaned down and kissed me gently.

But the adoration. It wasn't from me. It was his emotion making me feel so entirely loved for my whole being. "Do you feel that?" I asked.

"The astonishment that someone could love you so? Yes, I feel that."

I cocked my head. "But that's what I am feeling."

Rune smiled as he drew a finger along my tattoo. The skin beneath heated. "It's the bond. Ours is manifesting, so we feel the other's emotions. I felt it whenever we masked the caves." He pulled away from me and flipped onto his back.

I held my hand up, turned it. So the tattoo was never a fae bargain. I knew they formed with mate bonds, but that had never entered my mind. The Oracle and Vespa must have done something to make it appear earlier than it would have.

I rolled to my side to face him. The moonlight made his tanned skin glow.

Slowly he turned his face toward me. A lick of shadow snaked out from him and caressed my cheek. "I never thought this would be possible." His eyes roved over my features as his hand followed the path of his shadow as he rolled to face me.

"And why is that?"

"The idea of you. Of us. It's been lethal to me. Torturous. To want — need — someone so much, and she..." His fingers trailed down my neck, stilled as he gazed at me with open adoration.

I swallowed. Then finished his sentence for him. "She looked at you with hatred."

He nodded. Through the bond, I felt a reflection of how that had been for him, like he was the moth drawn to the flame only to get burned again and again.

I rolled, so I hovered over him. "Not anymore. You've shown me who you are, and now what do I look at you with?" Leaning forward, I placed a kiss on his lips, allowing myself to explore, to nibble, to tease.

When I pulled back, he murmured, "How is this possible?" as he drove his hands through my hair.

"We just went over this," I said with a flirty roll to my eyes.

"The whole fae-witch marriage thing escaped your notice?" His eyes twinkled with suppressed mirth.

I snorted. "No one seemed to care if fae and witch slept together."

His hand stilled, and I realized what I brought up. *Who* I brought up.

Landon. He was obvious before that he knew who I slept with.

"I cared," he whispered, not meeting my eyes.

I swallowed, not knowing what to say, cursing myself for being so careless with my words. "He meant nothing to me."

Rune's fingers tightened along my skin. "Don't."

I froze, my stomach sinking.

Rune's eyes met mine then. He must have seen something in my expression. "I mean, don't apologize. We had no claims on one another. But, Wall, was I insanely jealous." He chuckled. "Did you ever see him with that broken nose? It took a bit to heal." He laughed again.

"Were you responsible for that?" I slid a hand over his collarbone and down his chest, loving that laugh. I wasn't sure I'd ever heard it before.

"He wanted to spar, so I whole-heartedly obliged him. At the time, he asked me what the fuck was wrong with me." His eyes darkened and took on a faraway look before he pursed his lips and didn't continue.

"Well, what did you say? Did you admit it? Did he figure it out?"

"He didn't know. No one in the Summer Court knew how infatuated I was with you. If anything, I gave them the opposite idea..." he grimaced.

"Well played. I thought you hated me, too."

"Far from it. I knew you'd be my partner on this assignment, and the nerves I had. But I knew I couldn't reveal the truth until there was at least a chance you felt it too. That first night just about killed me. And after we about froze to death."

We both laughed until a seriousness came over us. Partially because I had rejected him that last time, but, for me, it was now the question that circled in my mind. The one he'd suggested. I snuggled into his side, letting my hand brush along his chest. "So what do we do now? We're bonded. It's treason."

"What's a bit more treason on top of what we already have done?" He paused. "We finish the assignment. We can't let Galwick win. This is crucial to the survival of the fae, of Cirrelea. We go from there."

"Day by day then."

He leant in to place a searing kiss on my lips. "Day by day. Side by side. Always."

ELEVEN

Sleep didn't come easily that night — mostly because we couldn't keep our hands off one another. It was a typical response to the new bond from what Rune said. But we both knew Galwick's men would be searching as well as any other of Faerie's creatures like the sluagh. Her body would tip off whatever creatures out there roamed, and they'd come looking. If another sluagh found it, they'd all come for revenge.

As much as we wanted to indulge the bond's wants, we got up the next morning after only an hour or two of actual sleep. After this cave, we only had the Summer Court cave to go. It would be the most dangerous. We talked about sifting to the Suhmerials to hide for a few days. Indulge our bond, throw off Galwick's men. Lull them into thinking perhaps we perished at the hands of Faerie's beasts.

But, no. With the sign of Rune's slowed healing, we needed to get this task done. Vespa had already given her life to the cause and likely the Oracle too.

We crept through the forest toward the cave location. Somehow, the trees always had brightly colored leaves on their limbs so that they constantly drifted down in the gentle breeze, creating a soft flutter. Thankfully, it helped cover the noise of our feet crunching along the pathways, grinding them into the dirt.

We arrived at the cave, without having seen or heard anything. It felt too easy.

"I don't like it," I said.

"Neither do I, but we're here. Stay on alert. Get the job done. I'll check for anyone hiding." Rune closed his eyes. He appeared to be meditating, but I knew he reached out with his fae senses. His eyes opened. "Nothing. Literally nothing. I don't even feel the heartbeat of a bird or squirrel."

The idea of nothing out there was stranger to me than the idea of some hulking beast in wait. "Should we do it or go?"

Rune cast a thoughtful gaze to the horizon. "We're here. I say we do it as fast as we can, and then I'll sift us away. I don't think any of this is going to get easier the more we wait."

I pressed my lips together, not liking it but not liking the idea of delaying more. The more we procrastinated, the more Galwick's men would amass. If we were fast, then we could get away before whatever our combined magic signaled. "Fast it is."

"Right. We hide the box, and then we run outside to mask the cave."

Inside, we quickly placed the box within some rubble. Rune crouched, ready for us to conceal it. "Ready?" I asked.

He nodded, reaching for my hand. His was warm and calloused. And I couldn't help my mind wandering to how they felt on my body. He flexed his fingers, pulling me to the present issue.

"I still sense nothing out there. Let's get this done." Rune reached into his pocket, pulling out the turquoise pebble Fenwyn had given him. "May as well take precautions." He cocked a brow at me.

I grinned. "Thank you, Fenwyn." With a lighter heart, I fed a bit of my magic into the pebble as Rune did. The world several feet away from us took on a foggy quality. His pebble had worked! We both let out a happy laugh, but time was of the essence.

I unspooled more witchery. Having done this spell twice now, it was easier to do it faster. Rune's magic came out to meet mine, and we wove them together. His hand tightened, and he grunted. "Quickly."

He must sense something. The lightheartedness I felt moments ago evaporated. Tension grew in my neck and shoulders. My nerves got the better of me, and I slipped up on a knot I wove.

"Something is coming. We need to finish," Rune said. His nerves evident in his voice.

With a quick look, the spell was fine. We'd done it.

Rune tugged me to my feet, and we rushed outside. Our bubble of hiding followed right along, tied to the pebble that was now back in Rune's pocket.

Nothing was outside, but Rune's emotions pounded in my head. Apprehension. Hesitation. Followed swiftly by determination.

"We finish this. Then we sift." His eyes held me as if I was precious to him, and the truth of it came down the bond.

We clasped hands and didn't waste a second. We wove with frantic energy, but the spell from the pebble winked out. It distracted both of us. We paused our work, and the stab of fear that Rune felt amplified my own. The hairs on the back of my neck stood up.

"Quickly," Rune said.

I seized my weave and began again. A blast of air forced us apart. Rune crashed and bounced off the semi-solid cave opening. I landed in the dirt and rock behind me. I grasped for my witchery, but arms snuck under mine, lifting me to feet. The fear that panged through me was too much, and the hold I had on my witchery slipped through my fingers. Rune's eyes went wide, and he lunged. Two of Galwick's men sifted right in front of him, appearing out of nowhere, and swung their swords at Rune. He dodged, and a sword of shadow thrust through one man's back.

I struggled against the grip on me, but my panic combined with Rune's had me nearly hyperventilating.

The swirly feel of sifting hit me. And the last thing I saw was Rune lunging for me, one hand outstretched, and the Galwick soldier still standing and swinging his sword at the opening Rune had left him.

THE SMELL HIT ME FIRST, ROILING MY ALREADY QUEASY BELLY, AND I KNEW where I was at once.

The Underneath.

The panic from Rune had subsided, but I had no time to question that. I reached out with my witchery, searching for a source of fire. The effort made my already sweating forehead worse and my head ache.

"Get her dosed," a man's voice said. One that I recognized all too well. I'd heard it many times.

Landon, my old lover.

My previous, very selfish, very bad lover.

I might be queasy and with no fire source, but my fighting skills were nothing to sneeze at. I swung my arm out, not yet able to see as my stomach lurched, but I connected with a groin, judging by the *oof* followed by a groan. It was satisfying. Too bad I didn't think it was Landon that I got.

"For fuck's sake. I'll do it," Landon growled before addressing the guard I'd whacked in the balls. "Get out of here."

His shadowy shape was only coming into focus as I squinted in the darkness. The swooping effects from sifting didn't help at all when he created a small ball of light which was unfortunately not made of fire.

No torches were lit either. They'd been ready for me. Landon rummaged in a pouch before producing a small vial.

Bonds of air wrapped around me as Landon grinned. His face finally becoming clear, framed by his long blond hair and his bright blue eyes sparkling. How I now hated that face. Once I had thought he was so beautiful: so opposite the one I thought I hated.

Landon drew close. "I know how much you like being called a 'good girl,' so how about you drink this with no issue?" He lifted his hand and let his fingers caress my cheekbone before trailing down my neck and over my breast. "And then maybe I can praise you again, just like we used to."

The bastard.

Humiliation roiled through me, hot and feral.

I struggled against the bonds, wanting to knock his hand away, but to no avail, as he had my arms trapped against my sides. Instead, I spat in his face. "Fuck you."

He sighed as he used two fingers to wipe the spit away from his eyes right before he lunged, gripping my hair and pulling my head back. Tendrils of air pried my jaw apart and slithered down my throat, causing me to gag. If he meant to do that, then the joke would be on him if I projectile vomited all over him.

He pressed the vial against my lips as he poured it into my open mouth. I wanted to spit it up, but his air bonds manipulated my tongue and throat. The bitterness of witch hazel filled my mouth followed by saliva, and he kept working my muscles to get me to swallow it all.

He leaned in, pressing his cheek against mine while his hand wrapped around my throat. "Good girl," he murmured into my ear. "That wasn't so hard, was it? Just imagine that throat trick of mine, and all the fun we could have with it." His fingers rubbed along my neck in an intimate way.

A low, feral growl ripped up my throat as revulsion tore through me. I struggled against his air bonds, but I still couldn't move. I wanted to scream *get away from me*, but his bonds still held my jaw, held *me* at his mercy.

"Perhaps if we have time, we can try it out later," he whispered into my ear before biting my lobe as his fingers tightened ever so slightly around my neck. He pulled away. "But for now, we have somewhere to be, love."

His air bonds retreated from my throat, my jaw, and my teeth clacked as I clamped my mouth shut. A heavy shudder went through me as I tried to heave in a breath.

The effects of the witch hazel set in quickly, fogging my mind. I wouldn't be able to reach my witchery for hours, and judging by this haze, they had figured out how to intensify it.

Air bonds released from my legs, and my chest tugged forward. Landon walked ahead of me. If I didn't follow, he'd let me fall on my face and then would drag me.

The Underneath was pitch black except for right around us where Landon held his ball of light, but he unerringly knew the layout of the warren.

I could still feel his air bonds in my throat, ghosts of them. The violation of it. How he'd so easily made my body do what he wanted it to do. Then I thought of the witches killed after Braidoc. How often people who had seen the bodies mentioned there was no fighting back.

I swallowed the hard lump in my throat.

"You're one of Galwick's assassins." He was the one who had mutilated all those others, and I'd willingly let him take me to bed. Bile crept up my throat as Landon turned, his white teeth gleaming in the light.

"At your service." He bowed. "Did you not know?" he asked as he turned and kept walking. "I thought you knew, but I guess I don't see how you would have known. I always figured Rune had told you. The way he would stare at you." He laughed, placing a hand on his stomach. "I think he thought he wasn't obvious about it." He chatted with me like we were old friends. "I mean, he never approached you. Was never seen with you, but how his eyes followed you around like he was some sort of lost, starving puppy. Well, it was then I knew I had to get in your bed. And you let me in so willingly, eagerly. Wall, how it must have roiled him. He only proved it when he broke my nose." He brought his fingers to his face. "But no matter with my fae healing. Worth it."

Now I really was going to be sick. "Why do you hate him so much?"

Landon side-eyed me. "He has what I want. Well, had." He chuckled. "Committing treason tends to knock one down a peg or two in Galwick's eyes. Now I'm the one Galwick relies on to get things done."

His grin was sickening. What had I seen in him?

We continued on in silence, thankfully. No more gloating from him, but his talk of Rune gave me the presence of mind to search for the bond.

It was there, taking space in a corner of my mind. It was comforting, like that space had always been empty before and now was full. But it felt distant. Not quite like a fog covered it, more like if I reached for it, it would take longer for me to grasp it, or maybe I wouldn't be able to reach it all without a lot of focus and exertion. I didn't know how these things worked, but if I didn't focus on it too hard, I could almost sense something. Determination. It was what I needed at the moment.

Rune was alive. He'd survived that other Galwick soldier. I was certain.

We exited the Underneath where I had entered it days ago, but it felt like months. Only now I knew why it was located there.

Right across the hall was the entrance to the Summer Court's dungeons. Landon grabbed my arm, but not quite tight enough to bruise. "See that you cooperate, and this will go much more easily for you."

Down the steps, we went into the dungeon. He led me through the area for the low-security prisoners. Wouldn't want to offend a rival court by putting any disorderly fae in the real dungeons. No, Galwick liked to present that he was civilized.

It was all a front.

Deeper and deeper we went, and fouler and fouler the stench became. But I held back a smile as it told me how much of a threat they thought I was. We passed the cells where prisoners were left to rot and even further past the light torture rooms. You only lost fingernails and maybe the whole finger in those, or so I'd heard.

We kept going to what I thought might be the bottom, where everything changed. No longer were there open cells with bars where prisoners could see each other and talk. Now it turned back to heavy iron doors, and the smell disappeared. It was almost sanitary. If nothing else, that part unnerved me. That and how the moans and screams of prisoners disappeared as soon as we entered, like the entire area had a privacy dome around it. And the way I felt nothing as I prodded for it...there had been witches who had to help with something for Galwick in the dungeons and later wound up dead.

Finally, Landon stopped outside a door, slipped a glove on, traced a rune on the door, and opened it. He tugged me inside. The room was black. Only light from the open door spilled in, high-lighting the iron chains that lay on the gray, smooth floor.

"You can hold still while I place these on you, or I can use my air bonds again and then have some fun." Air bonds slithered over my jaw, in between my teeth. There was no pressure to pry my mouth open, but the threat was there.

I held still as he grabbed one iron chain and clipped it around my ankle. It anchored in the corner of the room on the floor. The other was halfway up the wall with a smaller shackle. He clipped that one to my wrist.

"Where do I use the bathroom?" There was nothing in here. "Where do I sleep?"

Landon touched the shackle and whispered a word, and they tightened down, fitting snugly to my body before he stood. He drew a finger down my cheekbone, and I pulled away. "You're going to have much bigger things to worry about soon, and you'll no longer care about your dignity either. You can shit your pants for all we care." And with that he turned and left, the door closing behind him, leaving me in the pitch black, but not before I had the chance to make sure my tattoo was still etched on my arm.

TWELVE

Had it been hours? Days? I didn't know. I'd been dosed with witch hazel again, but if they concentrated the formula, then I had no idea how often I'd need it. My mouth was parched, and my stomach rumbled. The black room was neither too cold nor too warm. I lay sprawled out on the floor, which was blessedly clean as far as my hands could tell. No grime or dirt. Just smooth, cold flooring. I didn't even think it was rock.

I'd explored a bit. The chains allowed me to get almost to the other corners. The center of the room held a drain, which had given me some pause. But I already knew they wouldn't be kind to me here. Maybe they'd kill me. At least that meant I wouldn't have to burn.

I kept checking the bond. Rune was out there, somewhere. At one point, the intensity that I felt his emotion drastically changed. Did he sift and come closer, or were his emotions that much more? At least I knew he'd beaten that last Galwick soldier if I could still feel him or at the very least gotten away.

I rubbed my wrist where I knew the shared tattoo lay. That was the worst part of this sensory depravation. I couldn't see it. And seeing it would have brought me comfort. It was there when Landon had shut me in, but while time was the great healer of all things. It was also the great killer.

I'd read somewhere, maybe one of those fae romance novels the witches liked to pass around, that the fated mate tattoo would disappear if one of them died.

I rubbed down my arm again in hopes that I could feel it. But all I felt was my smooth skin.

The silence was loud. My ears rang with it. And when the door opened, I nearly jumped out of my skin, my eyes slamming shut at the sudden brightness.

Someone walked in with heavy steps which grew closer until they halted in front of me. I slowly blinked, allowing my eyes to adjust.

Maven, the apothecary, stood in front of me. He and I would sometimes chat when I'd come to deliver the herbs or pick up some potions for the life witches to use in conjunction with their witchery. Or even weapons like flasks which fire witches could toss to the ground to produce flame to channel from. How I wished I had those now.

He quickly created four balls of light and hung them in each corner of the room before the door behind him was allowed to close with a clank.

"Lily." He squatted down to speak to me as I struggled to sit up. "How are you this evening?"

He was so formal, so polite, acting like we had never conversed before, shared jokes. But maybe... "I'm starving, and I need water. Witch hazel isn't great on an empty stomach."

He smiled, a dimple popping up on his cheek. "It's your lucky day then because..." He paused, and the door opened, revealing someone standing there. They came in, a platter covered with a silver domed lid. I didn't need to see what was underneath. I could smell it. My mouth watered. It was as if they purposely picked the most delicious smelling breakfast foods.

Maven motioned for the other person, some court servant, to put the platter down by the door, an area I knew I couldn't reach in these chains. "If you answer my question this morning, I'll let you have the platter of food. Should we take a look to see what is on the menu?"

His mannerisms were so different from the Maven I knew. And my stomach sank.

I shook my head at his implied question. No. A sick feeling already filled me. I wouldn't answer anything, so that food would be better gone and out from under my nose.

"I see." He hummed. "It's a simple question right now. And really, you've got a number of things going against you." He leaned in, sniffing me. "One being that I smell Rune all over you." He tsked. "Naughty, but who am I to judge him for slumming it with a witch? Sometimes, if they're willing, then we may as well avail ourselves of them."

I swallowed my hate. How dare he? This was someone who had always seemed to treat me with friendliness. And now to know how he truly felt? I hated him. I narrowed my eyes as he stood, towering over me. How easily he had gone from acting friendly to interrogator.

"Let me begin with easing your mind that we know you didn't steal Lord Galwick's stone of Cirrelea. Vespa admitted to that before her death." He made a sad puppy face at me. "Apologies, if that is the first you are learning of that."

I said nothing. Only adjusted so that I now stood too.

He continued, "Nothing? I guess you had heard."

Irritation got the better of me. "What is your question?"

"So impatient. But since you asked. What I'd like to know is what did Vespa tell you to do? She gave you the stone. What did she tell you to do with it?"

"That's quite a question." I didn't know where this stupid bravado came from.

"Will you answer it—" he glanced behind him at the food "—for that?"

"No." Why would I? I knew where my loyalty lay, and it certainly wasn't here. I'd do what I could to protect my sisters, protect Rune. If that meant my life, so be it.

Maven lunged forward, grasping my chin and jaw with one bruising hand. "This could go so easily for you, you know? You just need to answer me."

"Why not ask the Oracle? Or did your truth serums not work on him?"

He hissed. The man literally hissed, throwing my head back with his hand. I narrowly missed bashing my head on the wall.

"Clearly you need more time to yourself." He spun around, kicked the platter of food out the door, and then let the door slam behind him, enclosing me once again in pitch black.

At some point, someone dropped broth and bread at the door. I had to use my feet to drag the tray close enough, spilling most of the broth. I knew they wanted me alive. It wouldn't be poisoned. The risk was some other sort of drug, but a few nibbles assured me it was clean.

Time passing was a non-issue. I had no idea. Seconds could be days. Days could feel like an eon. And every now and again, there was the slightest breeze. The only thing I could track was each time Landon came in to dose me with witch hazel.

I feared their method of torture was working. Sitting here waiting, doing nothing. I preferred the thought of them harming me over this. At least then I'd be angry and could fight back. I'd have some sort of satisfaction at spitting in their faces and denying them the knowledge they wanted to know. That Vespa or the Oracle hadn't broken was somewhat mollifying to me. If they could hold out, so could I. But for what? Would they just leave me here to rot?

And then I wondered if they wanted me to be bait. Bait to bring Rune in.

"Lily," a voice whispered, and it was so familiar, so known to me I wanted to cry.

"Rune!" I nearly sobbed. "Where are you?"

He was in my head. He had to be. Though we'd never spoken that way before. Rune had mentioned our bond manifested with our emotions, but I knew two fae mates could sometimes mind-speak.

"I'm close. What is it they want to know?"

My heart leapt at the sound of him. "How close? Do they have you?"

"Focus, Lily. What do they want to know?"

"What Vespa and the Oracle asked us to do."

"And have you told them?"

"No."

"Are they harming you?"

"Only withholding food."

He was silent, and I picked at the leather of my pants bunching at my knees.

"Rune! Where are you?" Even though my eyes were open, I only stared at the darkness.

"I'm here. Thinking…"

"I have to find a way out of here."

"What if you were to give them the answer they wanted…"

My breath stilled, as did my fingers. "You can't be serious. Tell them what they want to know?"

The silence from him felt weighty.

"It would keep you alive," he said on a whisper.

"I'd be alive, but in the dungeon. I can't believe you are telling me this. Are you free? Did they find you? Can you get me out?"

Nothing. My ears rang in the silence as my heart shivered as veins of ice enclosed around it.

"Rune?"

Landon unerringly showed his face. Always with the threat to do more with his air magic than force me to drink the witch hazel. I began to look forward to his visits. It was the only way I could tell any time. And the fog over my brain never lifted, my witchery encased in an impenetrable cloud along with my rapidly fading hope.

How could I escape? Rune hadn't contacted me again, and I was beginning to doubt that he had. Maybe my brain made it up.

Landon stood before me. This time, he left off the air bonds. As he brought the vial to my lips, his hand gently grazed down my cheekbone. I pulled away, and his eyes softened. I braced myself for a blow, but he only tipped the contents into my mouth. The witch hazel burned less than usual, likely from me now having taken it so many times. And then he left.

He must have knocked the hard hunk of bread I had left because the door didn't slam behind him.

Footsteps rang out, and I scooched forward as far as I could while holding the chain off the floor to not make noise.

"Have you broken her yet?" The voice sounded a lot like Lord Galwick.

"No, but Maven wants to give her more time on her own. Let her really see how screwed she is. No matter how lethal she thinks she is."

"Hmmm. We need to find him."

"He'll come."

"You sure about that?"

"I sent someone to check on the area where they captured her. Look for clues. Besides, Maven says she smells of him, and Landon claims he was in love with her. He'll be here soon, if not already."

"If you botched this one…" A sound rang out like flesh impacting flesh.

One set of footsteps rang out, clipped and angry, before fading away. A moment later, I heard scraping as if someone got up off the ground. His steps were hesitant and came toward my door, paused before the hunk of bread was kicked into the room and the door clicked shut.

But one split second before the door closed, my gaze met Landon's. And Goddess save me, something passed between us. He'd done that on purpose. But why?

Mind games.

It had to be.

I tried to not let it unsettle me. My thoughts — because that was all that kept me company — ricocheted around my head. It had to have been staged to make me believe Rune was alive. I knew he was, but they didn't know of our bond. Why would Landon want me to hear that conversation and make it clear he'd done that? And earlier he'd practically been kind. No snide remarks. Gentle with me.

A subtle breeze shifted my hair.

"Lily."

"Rune." I breathed out in relief, my heart lifting at just the sound of his voice. "Where have you been?"

"Have you thought on what I said?"

My mouth opened, but nothing came out.

"You're never going to get out of there unless you tell them what they want to hear."

Was this voice in my head or was it in the room? A shiver along my spine raised goose bumps. "Tell me what you have been doing."

"Trying to keep my head."

I frowned into the pitch black. From what I had just overheard, they had no idea where he was. Maybe he meant he was trying to figure things out, but something told me that wasn't it.

"Lily, they'll kill you."

Something was off. Rune wouldn't want me dead, but he wouldn't tell me to give them the answers they seek.

I didn't know who it was or how they were doing it, but it wasn't him. Even having just completed our mate bond, he wouldn't want me to give it all up. Do what I could to survive? Yes. But not give away what we knew would save Cirrelea one day.

"Then they'll kill me," I said, my voice hard.

He didn't speak again.

THIRTEEN

Hours later, the door opened, and Maven entered. Again, someone followed behind him with a platter of exceptionally pleasant-smelling food. This time he lifted the dome and pulled out a long thin piece of meat, fried to perfection and crunched on it in front of me. "Mmmm."

The bastard. Food was a way to break me. My stomach growled loud enough to make him chuckle. "Tired of broth and bread yet?"

"Never," I said, turning away from him.

"Landon," he called out. "Looks like I have need of you."

Landon appeared in the doorway. For someone with such perfect features, the way the light lit him from behind, he seemed absolutely menacing.

Instinct had me scooch back towards the Wall that held the anchors for my chains, and Landon's face tightened.

"Light," Maven said.

Landon sent a few balls of light to the corners of the room, making me blink back tears. I'd been in the dark so long and only ever getting the dim light that poured in through the door when opened. This light was too bright.

Maven prowled before me. "Give her the serum before we begin."

Serum? Not witch hazel?

Landon's air bonds swept over me, pulling me to a kneeling position and pushing my head back and opening my mouth, but it wasn't like Landon over the past few days. Landon always used his air bonds on my body like he owned me. This was different, almost reverent. And after earlier? How he'd let me hear the conversation?

Now he stood over me, which was too reminiscent of past times. The way his legs spread apart, how he ran a hand over my brow and into my hair. But again, juxtaposed with a gentle touch. Like he cared.

I met his eyes with all the hatred I could muster into them, but his were only full of something I couldn't name. It made my stomach swoop.

Before I could make sense of it, Maven growled. "Stop screwing around and get on with it. She needs to get that serum in her."

Landon cleared his throat as if Maven's words brought him back to his senses. Then he smirked, and my throat spasmed, swallowing on nothing but fear. He uncorked a different bottle and poured it down my mouth before backing away.

I gagged, but he used his air to close my mouth. With my eyes, I told him how much I hated him. Again. What I saw earlier be damned.

"Good. Now that is taken care of. Let's get down to business. You seem to lack the motivation to tell us what Vespa and the Oracle told you to do. That is why I am here. To motivate you. Or shall I say, that is what the serum is for."

The taste in my mouth confirmed that what Landon gave me was definitely not witch hazel. There was no bitterness. The last witch hazel had tasted less than usual, but this was sweet. Yet, Rune had mentioned my shipments of primrose to Maven for the truth serum, and what I just took didn't taste anything like primrose. It was more like my standard cough remedy. Landon released the air bonds on my jaw as my thoughts scattered in my head. I held fast to one thing. Primrose may be in this serum, and I may not taste it at all. Anyone who had been around crafting remedies or potions knew much could be added to mask a foul taste. I rolled my neck, trying not to show how much Maven's words made my heart jump. This was it.

"How about now you tell me what I want to know." He leaned down to say the last bit in my face, his breath moving my hair.

"Or?" I gritted out.

"Or…" he smiled, "we'll just wait a bit longer for the serum to take effect. But if you wait for the serum, you'll never get out of here." He stood up, lifting a brow.

Shock rolled through me. Rune had said something almost exactly the same a bit ago, but I couldn't let it show. "I don't think I'll get out of here either way, so…" I lifted a shoulder. "May as well wait and see if your little concoction works. It clearly didn't work on the Oracle or Vespa."

Maven made a sound with his teeth before he lunged at me. He pulled my hair back as he raged in my face. "You'll burn for this."

"Then the answer will burn with me," I grated out even as my back arched painfully.

"You leave me no choice."

As much as I told the fear swelling within me to leave, that it had no place here, an unease crept along the edges. Not fear, a blackness. Maven gripped my chin and stared into my eyes. I didn't know what he was doing. I pulled back, but he held fast.

The black on the edges intensified and felt like someone peeling my mind like a citrus fruit. I yanked back, pulling out of Maven's grip as his eyes stared off into the distance.

"Landon, hold her steady."

Air bonds formed all around me, but they held me looser than normal. My gaze flicked to Landon, who stood stoic and with what looked like hatred in his eyes. But he looked at Maven.

It was odd, but I had no time to consider it as someone rushed in and whispered in Maven's ear, causing him to straighten and turn quickly. He grabbed Landon by the arm, and both left. The bonds evaporated from around me. And the door slammed shut.

Silence enveloped me. What in the Wall?

I assessed myself. Besides my scalp slightly stinging still from Maven's grip on my hair, I didn't feel any different. If anything, I felt less foggy. Would I feel the serum working? Would it lift the fog concealing my witchery from me?

The answers to my questions would have to wait. I had to figure something out.

Landon's balls of light still hung around the room. Light was not fire — certainly not from Landon — but they had a kernel of something in common. I stood and jumped, trying to grab at one. If I had one, hid it, and they lapsed on witch hazel, then maybe, just maybe, I could tap into my fire witchery. It would be small, but it would be something.

I kept jumping, kept trying, not even caring that the chains made a racket. No one came to the door. With the two of them rushing out like they did, I doubted anyone was out there. Something was happening. Maybe it was Rune, so I had to be ready.

My legs tired. I gasped for breath with my hands on my knees, and my gaze connected with the anchor in the wall for my leg. That might just give me enough height to reach the one ball of light.

It was worth a shot. And it would certainly hold my weight. I climbed on top. It barely fit both my feet. But I only needed it for a second. I pushed with all my might, willing myself to reach the ball. My fingers touched it, but it was like grasping something that would ooze through your fingers. Solid, but not. My feet hit the floor.

The good news was that I'd moved it and pushed it down to where I could reach it without having to jump.

I stretched and gently cupped it with both hands, herding it closer to me. It was warm, comforting. Totally unlike its creator.

But what to do with it now that I had it? Keeping it on me, under my clothes was never going to work. They'd see it as soon as they came in. Even my leathers wouldn't hide it.

Then an idea struck me, and I had no idea what it would do to me. But I didn't have time for doubts. They could come back any second.

Keeping my hands cupped, I gently guided it to my mouth.

I swallowed it, hoping to Faerie that it wouldn't kill me, and that I wouldn't be glowing after.

It slid down my throat. For a moment, I gagged, choked. But then it was done, and relief flooded through me.

No glowing stomach. All good.

Unease slithered around me. Had I just made the worst decision of my entire life? What would Landon's magic do to me? Would he be able to sense it? What if he called them all back?

It didn't matter because as soon as I resumed my spot on the floor, the door opened.

Maven stalked in with an I-want-to-punch-him-in-the-throat smirk. "Seems like your partner is dead."

My heart stalled. "My...partner?"

"Rune."

No. No. No. This couldn't be. I would know, wouldn't I? I'm his mate. Aren't they supposed to know if something like that happened?

I reached out with my mind as my chest tightened and my heart raced. But that kernel of him was there. It felt like all tension, like someone completely focused on a task at hand and coiled like a snake ready to strike.

But they couldn't know how their news affected me. Indicating I cared for him would be folly. So I smiled. "Well then, I guess you're down to me and the Oracle for answers. And I don't intend to give them."

Maven's lip curled.

But I wasn't done. "I want proof. How do you know he is dead?"

Maven didn't move, but with the door to my cell open, I could hear boots on the floor and something being dragged.

Landon backed into the small room, dragging a body.

Rune's body.

He dropped it, and then I was staring at Rune's face with dead eyes.

Every muscle in my body went taught. I couldn't help it. As much as my mind screamed *hide it*, it also screamed in anguish at the sight of that beloved face. My bond told me one thing, but Rune's body in front of me said another.

My eyes welled with tears, and my lip quivered. I tried to hold it back, but I couldn't stop staring into Rune's dark eyes.

Maven crouched down, craning his neck to see me. "You cared for him?" He dragged the back of his index finger along my cheek. "How touching, and how disgusting." His voice went hard, dangerous. "A witch caring for a fae?"

I glanced down Rune's body, ignoring Maven. Something was amiss. He didn't seem broad enough. Was it just the way Landon had dropped him?

Maven stood, giving Rune's body a good kick with his foot. Rune's hand flopped to the ground, exposing the underside of his wrist.

No tattoo.

My heart squeezed. My tattoo had been there the last time I had looked. But they were supposed to disappear if our bond broke, if one of us died.

I grit out, "Where did you find him?" Let them see my sorrow. I extended my arms over my knees to rub my eyes. But I did it for show, to hide that I was looking at my wrist.

The tattoo was still inked into my skin, and I rolled my forehead against my palms to hide my smile.

It wasn't him.

"We found him where we found you. For an assassin, we got the two of you quite easily."

I didn't respond. I only put my head down onto my knees. I had no idea how Rune had accomplished this, but he had.

And his message was clear. *I'm alive. You stay alive.*

So that only left why he'd told me to tell them what we were up to, but given what Maven had said earlier and him trying to get into my mind, I wasn't sure if that had been Rune either.

Maven knelt again. "So guess what this means? Fun time is over. The serum has had plenty of time to work now, and since it doesn't seem like you're any more willing to give up answers, then I'll fetch them myself. Too bad. When I do that, people's brains tend to be mush after." He turned. "Landon, get him out of here. I can't stand to see him even if he is dead."

Landon strolled in, eyeing me. He leaned down to grab the body with Rune's face. But it was awkward. He pulled his leathers on his arms up, flashing me a tattoo.

On the underside of his wrist.

His eyes met mine. Held my gaze for a second, before he pulled the body away.

I checked in with the bond. It was awash in love and determination.

And rage.

My eyes widened. I wanted to rush to him, hold him. Something. Anything. But I couldn't do any of that. I still wasn't entirely sure how this bond worked, but I did the only thing I dared. I sent love and relief through my end, so he knew I recognized him.

A split second of comfort came from him before he shut it down.

I did the same. The emotions all the time that weren't my own could be distracting, overpowering.

Rune dragged the body out, and Maven paced in front of me. "Bring that next dose of witch hazel too! Can't have her even thinking she can fight me."

Rune was gone for a minute and came back with a stoppered bottle in his hand. He approached, and my heart pounded.

Shit. This couldn't be. Doubt filled me. I opened the bond.

Trust and love flowed through.

Rune with Landon's face stood over me, threatening. He grabbed my jaw, putting pressure on. I opened willingly, hoping I was right.

"No air this time?" Maven asked.

Rune curled Landon's face in a sick sneer. "I think she knows to be a good girl right now." He directed his attention to me. "Isn't that right? We had some fun earlier, and I *trust* you know what will happen."

I nodded as much as I could, not really having to pretend I was scared as my eyes darted from Maven to Rune. Wall, please let it be Rune.

He unstoppered the bottle using his teeth and poured it down my throat.

Not witch hazel. Something else.

"Swallow, just like earlier," Rune crooned. He stroked my face, but his gaze held mine with intensity, willing me to understand something.

But what?

I racked my brain. What did he want me to do?

He backed away, taking up a position behind Maven. But without Maven watching him, he relaxed. No, not relaxed. He hunched a bit, a hand to his side.

Pain seared through the bond. He was injured. To have Landon's face meant he was glamouring himself, and I knew that wasn't his main specialty in magic. He'd glamoured that other body to look like him. He had no more Source left or was dangerously low if he was taking a chance like this.

My mind began to clear.

He'd given me some sort of anti-witch hazel.

So it was up to me to use what he'd just given me.

Maven moved to stand in front of me. He spread his legs out as he pushed his index fingers against my temples. I reached out with my witchery. There was nothing. They had this cell locked down. I couldn't reach past the surrounding wards. But I had the light balls from Landon earlier, and I had the one in me. They would have to do.

I wouldn't be able to move the lights without Maven noticing.

His eyes were open, and I had no idea if he was in a trance or not. The risk wasn't worth it.

So the light in me is what I had to work with.

Rune's eyes kept flashing to the lights. I knew what he wanted me to do. Was it possible those lights were his? Was that him earlier?

I sensed the magic in me. It felt odd to be there.

Something slithered along the edge of my mind. My heartbeat ratcheted up. Maven.

I couldn't take forever. If I waited too long, Maven could potentially sense what I was doing. Read my mind. To me, he had been an apothecary, but he was so much more if he had mental powers.

I had to do something, so I tried to channel from the light. Nothing.

It was different. It called to me.

It was Rune's, and my mate bond recognized it as his.

Instead of trying to pull from it, I sent my magic toward it, like we did just before we joined our magics. His magic bubbled beneath mine, transforming.

It writhed as if heated. My fire with his power. But I couldn't hold it. It was growing too much, heating too much. I couldn't contain it, certainly not in me. I was going to sear my insides.

My instincts told me to do something I would have never dreamed of.

I breathed it out.

Fire spilled out of my mouth right at Maven in front of me. Right at his crotch where he had so helpfully positioned himself.

He yelped, dropping his hands, grabbing his balls and falling to the floor.

I took the opportunity to dive my witchery into another ball of light. I brought it close to him, and this time, since it wasn't literally in me, I let it burble and explode right next to his face.

He screamed, grabbing now at his face, his eyes. Wicked burns seeped all over his exposed skin.

I let my witchery dive into another ball of light as Rune lunged at Maven and drove a dagger into his heart.

Rune stood, grinning at me before coming close and brushing the hair from my face. "That was absolutely amazing. Absolutely lethal of you." And even though I knew it was him, he still wore Landon's face, which tamped down on my elation.

I jangled my chains, anxious to be free of them. He fished into his leathers. "I have a key."

Once I was free, Rune pulled me in for a kiss, but I braced myself on his chest.

"What's wrong?" he murmured.

"Not with his face."

Understanding shone through his eyes. "Well, I can't remove his face for now. We need to get you out of here."

"How'd you know what Maven meant by the air from Landon?"

Something dark fluttered across his features. "Let's just say Landon and I were sometimes both assigned to make a prisoner talk. I knew his methods, especially with females. Now, hold your hands together in front of you. You'll look my prisoner. Only two people would dare question us, and one of them is dead." He spared a glance at Maven, giving him a solid kick to the ribs. "I wish I could have made it a slow death for him." A grin spread across his face. "But I'll never forget you roasting his cock off. Worth it."

He grabbed my arm and led me out of the cell, locking the door behind us. If, by some chance, Maven healed, then he wouldn't be able to get out. Not to mention it hid his body.

"You're injured," I said as low as I could, having no idea what kind of guards were around.

"My source is low. Holding those glamours for as long as I did drained it right out of me."

"You need to rest. What do we do now? Where are we going?"

Rune cast me a cocky look. "I'm Landon. I'm bringing you to my quarters to have my way with you." He waggled his brows.

The whole thing was so odd. His voice. Landon's face. "Ugh, don't do that. Not with his face on."

Rune led us toward the dungeon entrance I knew, but instead of heading toward the steps out, he walked toward what I thought led to a guard room. Once inside, a tingling sensation skittered along my skin. My witchery told me it was from around the one door. An illusion was here but made by witches, to hide that door. I could see it, but fae wouldn't be able to. My stomach turned. Another example of how my brothers and sisters were used and cast away by Galwick.

"Now you know one of the Summer Court's greatest secrets," Rune said.

"And that is?"

"Galwick's assassins would be fairly easy to assassinate if you came in through the dungeons."

And the Underneath brought one right to their entrance.

"But I doubt you all made it easy."

He snorted. "Yes, well, needless to say, none of us liked how the Underneath exposed us. So we booby-trapped this entire area. And frankly, they likely un-keyed me from all of it. So mind your step."

Mind my step?

Rune stepped forward, then pointed down. A tripwire of the thinnest steel lay a few inches above the stone floor. If you weren't looking for it, it'd blend in perfectly with the grey stone.

After stepping over it, Rune moved further down the hall. "Can you fight fire with fire?"

"No."

"Right then, on to our stomachs."

Worming our way forwards felt ridiculous. "How many more of these are there?"

Rune stood after a few feet of crawling. "One more, but they hadn't changed those two, and I'm a bit worried this last trap is."

"What was it?"

"Pressure plates that release gas." He scanned the floor.

Surely he could identify that even if they had moved it.

"Can you tell?"

He shook his head.

Down the hall, the corridor ended in a T-junction. A door opened and closed. One of Galwick's personal guards rounded the corner and took a few steps in before stopping short, registering we were there.

"Ah, Landon." His eyes flicked to me and clouded with suspicion. "What are you doing here?"

Rune slid a hand around my bicep. "Maven's done with this one for a bit, so I thought I'd have a bit of fun, if you know what I mean." He squeezed.

I jerked my arm, glaring back at him, playing the part. "You can't do this."

Rune grinned wickedly. "Oh, love, but I can."

The guard stepped closer. "Then what are you waiting for?"

Rune pushed me into the zone he had been scanning and my entire body froze.

But nothing happened.

"Nothing," Rune said, "Just having a bit of fun with her. I told her it was a trap and was going to shove her into it."

The guard smirked as he nodded. Clearly he approved of Landon's ways. "Wasn't she one you used to visit?"

Rune tugged me back toward him. A hand came to my waist and his fingers gripped. "Do you have anything of substance to say?" He prodded me along, passing the guard until we were out of the trap zone.

The guard went on his way, muttering something about assholes while Rune fished in his pocket for a key ring. "I never thought I'd be thankful for that guy, but either providence smiled upon us or we are the luckiest to ever live," he muttered as he found the key and inserted it into the lock.

The door swung open, and we entered Landon's room. I'd never been here before. All our trysts had been in my quarters or a hidden place somewhere in the court.

"Now for that injury," I said. "Let me look."

"Alas, if I drop the glamour, I may never get it back."

"If *you* die, I may never get *you* back. Drop the glamour."

He sighed, and Landon's blonde hair morphed to his deep brown locks before he collapsed to the bed.

"Where is Landon?" I asked.

"In one of the empty cells near where you were." Rune struggled to get out of his leathers as I searched for any kind of healing kit. "His desk, right side."

Landon, for such a scummy fae, was actually meticulous in his quarters. Even his weapons were all perfectly arranged. What a psycho.

I strode toward the desk, pausing as I reached for a drawer. "You knew him well?"

Rune snorted. "I wouldn't say well. He was good with a needle. Very orderly and precise."

The drawer slid open, and a pouch sat on top of everything else, filled with needles, bottles, bandages, and dried herbs.

I brought the bag over to Rune, who groaned as I sat down on the bed, and got my first good look at his injury, a stab wound to the side.

"He wasn't the easiest to kill once he realized I was an enemy. I had the edge of surprise, but he got one lucky swing in. At least it wasn't poisoned." He tipped his head back as I felt around. "I don't think he hit anything major."

I hummed. "A flesh wound, looks like." I poked around in the bag and found the herbs I wanted.

A kettle hung in the fireplace over dead coals. No matter. Up here, I had my witchery. I channeled from outside torches to heat the water to a boil and dropped the herbs in. "We'll clean it, stitch it, then I'll make a poultice to bandage it."

I sat, waiting for the herbs to steep. "How are we going to finish this? How will we get out?"

"After, they sifted with you." He groaned as he shifted. "I sifted my way back to Fenwyn and Muriel. They'll finish the spell to obscure the cave. I didn't know who would come back to visit the scene."

"Someone checked."

Rune grinned. "That was me. I glamoured the body of the one guard to look like me and took his identity. I killed the guy they sent to look, then took his face."

"You have shadows and water, don't you?" As an assassin, those were both skills to have, but no one seemed to know he had skills in water.

"Even Galwick didn't know I had water. It's not strong like my shadows, uses more Source, but the glamour aspect of it has been useful, and for the occasional witch who likes to throw daggers made of flame."

"How did Galwick not know?"

He grimaced as he picked a bottle up off the night stand, sniffed it and place it back. "My strength in water came later. I was with the Oracle — he must have known, seen it — but he sat me down, wagged his finger about and told me no one could know. That there was only one person I could trust with this information. My fated. He said if Galwick knew, then he'd use me even worse than he would with only my shadow magic. As you said, the two combined make me lethal. And I've really only used it while escaping. Until now. I couldn't risk the rumor getting out. If it did, Galwick would have had me tested."

It was not unheard of for a fae to have superior strength in another tree of magic, but it was rare. And historically speaking, those with strength in two trees of magic within the Summer Court weren't treated well. The potential for either being seen as competition or that they were a weapon to be wielded was always there. The Oracle hadn't been wrong.

"So Fenwyn and Muriel will finish our spell on the cave? We'll have to deal with the Summer Court one then."

"Yes, I couldn't ask them to do that one too. I put them in even more danger than they've put themselves in by staying together."

"And the journal—"

"In my Rift."

The aroma of the herbs grew strong, so I poured a bit out to cool. "So, we have one court left and then we can get our next set of instructions." *Please don't let it be placing anything else all over Cirrelea.*

Rune stayed silent long enough to make me glance at him to be sure he was still conscious.

"I think once I am strong enough to rift the journal back, we burn the map and get the final instructions."

I tested the heat of the tonic to let his words sink in. Burning it. Telling it we had finished all four courts. "That's genius." It was exactly what we needed to do. Because we had to know what was next. Especially if we got to the cave and had to make a break for it.

I turned to Rune with my cooled tonic and clean bandages, pouring some of it on his wound, making him hiss and then dabbing it up. The cloth quickly turned red. The bleeding had slowed, his fae healing still doing its job. Next I grabbed the needle, threaded it and got to work. Rune stoically took it, a testament to what conditions he must have come back in to still need it when his fae healing wasn't stifled.

"You said the slower healing was a new thing. How has it changed from ages ago?"

Rune shifted on the bed. "It's related to our source. If we are low, healing is slowed. If I am at full capacity, I can hardly tell the difference. But it wasn't always that way."

And these past days he'd been chronically low on source. His eyes slid shut, and I used more tonic on the stitches then ground up some herbs with some oils from Landon's bag and wrapped his wound as he nodded off.

I rummaged in the room for anything of use: food, more healing herbs and bandages, weapons. Anything to keep my mind off still being in this court and being so close to being free but having to bide my time.

Rune slept soundly. I had told him one hour. He needed it, but neither of us thought we could risk more.

Once I was done collecting things, I sat in the chair, watching Rune's chest rise and fall. It gave me time to finally mull over what I had done in that cell.

I'd transformed Rune's light, and it had grown both in size and intensity. And it hadn't attracted attention like when we joined our magics crafting our own spell. But one thought kept circling in my mind. If I could transform his magic outside his body, what about inside his body? And had I already done it? When we'd had sex, I'd touched his source with my witchery. Perhaps I could help him recover more than what an hour's rest would give him.

FOURTEEN

I gently nudged his arm, caressed his face, kissed his lips. His arms slid around me. "Keep that up, and we won't be leaving yet."

I smiled against his lips but pulled back. As much as I'd love to have that with him again, we needed to get out of Galwick's court, certainly out of his castle. "I have an idea. How are you feeling?"

"I can Rift the journal, but a full glamour of Landon again?" He grimaced.

"Let's get the journal, then I'll tell you my idea."

The journal appeared in Rune's hand as I laid beside him. Earlier, I'd put a plate of some sort of cookies Landon had stashed away by the bedside. Rune nibbled on them as he handed the book to me..

I flipped through all the instructions, making sure we hadn't missed any. "Map?"

Rune rifted the map. I committed the location of the Summer Court cave to mind. It might be all we had. I channeled my witchery, hoping this wasn't a bad idea, and set the map alight as Rune held the journal so we could both see. Words began to appear on the first empty page.

Congratulations, you have completed the main task, and Cirrelea is far safer now than it had been. Faerie owes you a debt of gratitude, but not all the residents may feel the same.

The words took forever to appear. Rune rolled to his non-injured side to curl around me.

Your job, however, is not complete. The stone must leave Cirrelea to be safe. For Cirrelea to be safe.

Rune and I exchanged a glance. Leave Cirrelea? How?

The Wall. There is a way to pass through. The fae source we left you — which we are sure raised your eyebrows. We hope you still have it. We hope we spared you having to take one, find one of your own. It was the least we could do.

Insert it into the stone. You must be linked physically to each other while one of you holds the stone. Cross through.

This journal will know when you are on the other side and will have everything else you need to know. Say your goodbyes to Faerie. And welcome the companionship we hope you have found in one another, as we found in one another.

Well, shit.

My worries about what we will do once we've completed our mission were for naught. The Oracle and Vespa always knew we wouldn't be staying here.

"So they sent us on this mission, knowing they would banish us in the end?" Rune sat up, groaning with a hand at his side.

I reached out for him. "Careful. Is it feeling better?"

He tried to keep the wince off his face, but I saw it anyway.

"Still hurts like a baedour's bite, but it feels better than it did." He lifted a hand to caress my cheek, "Thank you." After a moment, he looked away, something clouding his eyes. Anger came through the bond.

"What is it? We'll be safer over there."

His eyes slid back to mine. "We hope. Humans are over there. The same humans who wanted to kill us ages ago."

Us. Him. Fae. I stifled my knee-jerk reaction to be mad.

"That's what they say. But they burned all that history ages ago. And why would one do that?" I raised a brow.

"You're right, but why wouldn't they just tell us we were leaving Cirrelea to begin with?

"Maybe because if we knew, we wouldn't have agreed."

Rune drove a hand through his hair before snatching another cookie off the plate. "What's this idea of yours? Because I could glamour my face to look like Landon, but that's it. In a pinch, I might be able to muster more."

"Remember how I breathed fire?"

"How could I forget?"

"That was your magic. I think that is why I could do that. I didn't channel from it. I combined mine and yours, transformed it. What if I did that to you, your source?"

Rune froze with the cookie partway to his mouth. "You want to mess around with my source?"

"Well, say it like that, and it sounds bad."

I got off the bed, stood in front of him. "I promise I won't just dive in and start mucking about. Besides, I've already done it before. In the Autumn Court hut."

He deadpanned stared at me until I reminded him of that night and a sexy smirk spread across his lips.

"I promise. Trust me."

An emotion I couldn't name flickered across his face. An assassin wouldn't trust easily.

"Vespa told me to trust you. I can only assume the Oracle told you to trust me."

"I do. It's just..." He shut his eyes as if in pain.

But I finished his thought for him. "You don't trust easily. People you put faith in hurt you."

He nodded without opening his eyes. "Even the Oracle in the end. By not telling us everything."

So I slid my hands along his cheeks, tilting his chin up. "Look at me. I won't hurt you. Open your bond."

I had been prodding, but he'd been keeping it shut, probably to spare me the pain he was in.

The bond opened, filling me with love. He opened his eyes, his hands going to my waist, pulling me close.

No words were needed. The bond conveyed it all. He loved me. He trusted me.

"But what about how joining our magic always seemed to send out some sort of pulse?" he asked.

"It only seemed to occur when we were casting a spell together."

He nodded and pushed his power out. I met it with a thread of mine. The two twirled and twirled. We lost ourselves in the joy of it for a moment. In wonderment of how something so pure and awe-filled could be banned. Treasonous.

We were becoming one. I led my magic closer and closer to his, showing him what I could do. Little sparks flew between his thread and mine. His magic called to me. It was becoming against my nature to pull my magic away from his. The urge to fully unite them was nearly overwhelming.

But I had to let him see, had to let him see it was ok. I let the tip of my thread touch his. And in that conjoined spot, the magic flared, powerful and vibrant. I pulled mine away even though I didn't want to, and he made a tsking sound.

"Watch." I did it again but allowed more to touch. Again, it grew and flared. Together, our powers strengthened the other's.

"It's beautiful. You're beautiful," he said on a breath.

"Are you ok?" I threaded my fingers with his, holding our hands between our chests.

"I'm ok. Just have a look. Go slow." His thumb rubbed along mine.

I pulled my magic from his, and his thread of magic reluctantly spooled back into his source. Slowly I sent my thread of witchery to where I'd last seen his thread. I couldn't see his source, but I could sense it. I threaded around the outside of it ever so delicately.

He groaned, not in pain, in pleasure. "Wall, I've never felt anything like that."

Brazened by his reaction, I allowed my witchery to trail even closer, more than a feather-light touch.

He groaned again, releasing our hands and pulling me in tight against him so I could tell what it was doing to him. Warmth bloomed in my core. My hands trembled as I coasted them over his shoulders, down his bare arms.

"I'm going to try a bit more if you're ok with that."

"Wall, yes, if it keeps feeling this good, you can consume it."

I threaded a net around his source now, instinct guiding me. I'd have to leave some of my witchery with him for this to work and stay.

He groaned again and his hands dove to my ass, grinding me against him as he leaned over and kissed along my neck.

He was going to break my focus. I tightened the net down carefully. His hands now tugged at my clothes. And somehow I was helping and shedding them even as I watched how his source flare to life, growing, pulsating with power under my witchery.

His movements became frantic, pulling at fussy buttons and stuck stays, pushing me back onto the bed. His hand diving between my legs.

Now I was the one groaning and writhing. I kept tightening the net around his source, merging my witchery with him. Making them one.

"Lily, I...I desperately need you."

I had a leg still in my pants. My hands dove to his belt. Undid it, releasing him. "You can have me. I'm yours."

He pressed his forehead to mine, both of us coming back to the present for a moment. "You have no idea how long I've wished for those words from your mouth."

He grabbed my legs hooking them over his shoulders before he plunged in. His source throbbed beneath my witchery.

"Can you feel it, Lily? Can you feel what you're doing to me? You make me feel like a God. Together we are Gods."

I was so close. Neither one of us could hold out much longer. Somehow this conjoining of our magic was working our bond too, making us both feral with need for the other.

Something in me told me to tie off the witchery. I wove the knots to keep my net around his source before I lost all focus.

Rune pounded into me. Through the bond, I felt his pleasure. All his desperate want and need of me through the years being fulfilled. I felt how my witchery strengthened him. The wound in his side now merely a slight cut, the strength of his source renewing his ability to heal.

He chanted my name. And as we both went over the crest, he whispered. "You were the only thing that kept me alive all those years. Just the dream of you. The dream of this. I couldn't give up if there was even the slightest chance."

FIFTEEN

We didn't have the luxury to bask in the rose-gilded haze of lovemaking as much as we wanted to. Rune got me a cloth, cleaned me up then himself as we put our clothes to rights.

"How do you feel?" I asked.

He smirked.

I rolled my eyes. "Your power?"

"I feel..." He closed his eyes. "I feel like I have more power than I've ever had."

He snapped his fingers, and he was Landon. Clothes, stature, everything. He did it again, and he was Rune, my Rune.

I giggled. "Ok, well, don't waste it all."

"It feels like doing that is barely a drop out of the bucket. This is amazing." He pulled me toward him, laying a deep, sensual kiss on me before whispering, "You're amazing."

Someone pounded on the door.

We froze.

A voice spoke from the other side. "Landon? Do you still have the witch?"

He looked at me, and I took the cue. "Get your hands off me! You've had your way twice now. No more!" I threw as much fear and spite into my voice as I could.

"What do you need? Can't you tell I'm busy?" It was eerie how he could even make himself sound like Landon.

"You seen Maven?"

"Ah, fuck Maven. You know how he hides."

"Yes, but he was scheduled to meet Galwick. He never misses those."

Rune and I shared a look. I grabbed the small pack I'd packed earlier. Threaded the daggers into my leathers. Rune watched me and glamoured them so they disappeared from anyone else's eye as soon as I had them secured.

Rune grabbed his things before he whispered, "Get dressed. I guess our fun is done." Then shouted toward the door, "Give me a sec."

We shuffled around. Rune motioned with his hands to remind me to keep my wrists together.

Once we were both ready, he opened the door, looked the guard up and down before he drove a dagger into a weak point in the man's armor. With a hand on the back of the man's neck, hooking under the metal plate, he tossed the dying man into the room. We left and locked the door behind us.

"We need to get out of here. They'll look for Maven in your cell any moment now, if not already."

"So the Underneath is off limits to us to escape?"

"The Underneath is most definitely off limits. It's the first place they'll be looking and seeing you in there won't do."

"So how? Just out the door? Couldn't you just glamour me to look like someone else?"

An alarm rang out in the castle. Rune frowned. "I think we'll be taking a much less pleasant way out. I can glamour you, but I don't know another woman's face well enough to do it convincingly.

Besides, that personal guard of Galwick's knows you're with Landon. But you do need one thing to make this somewhat believable."

A tingle spread over my head, my cheeks.

"Don't touch your face. It'll show the glamour too easily. I'm not adept enough at things like trickling blood to have it work if your hand is in the way."

I reached up and Rune pursed his lips as if saying, *What did I just say not to do?* But it was only him and I. And I was still reeling from him admitting he had no other woman's face committed to memory.

"Did you make it look..." I trailed off as my fingers tapped along my temple, feeling nothing but smooth skin.

Rune nodded with Landon's face. "He liked to rough up a lot of the women he was with."

I swallowed and wouldn't meet Rune's eyes because he was Rune, because he wore Landon's face. Disgust slithered through me. I wanted to wash away that I'd ever let Landon touch me.

"Close your eyes."

I did as asked, and Rune stepped close. His scent washed over me. The bond pulsed with his love for me. "I'll make sure you don't ever remember his touch again. My touch will be the only one you'll ever think of." He coasted his fingers over my cheek, but he must have known kissing me with Landon't lips would be too much.

I sighed and nodded with a small smile on my lips as I opened my eyes. "I'm ready. Let's go."

Rune led us into the hall before pausing in front of one of the other doors in the short corridor.

"My old room."

"Do you want anything from inside?"

He gave a curt jerk of his head. "No. I have everything that means something to me." With a squeeze to my hand, he tugged me to the hall that met with the main part of the castle. Not the hidden, trapped corridor we came in by.

Rune grabbed my bicep, and I kept my wrists together in front of me. The alarm blared out again. A guard ran past and skidded to a halt.

"Landon! Where have you been?" The guard's eyes flicked to me and understanding flashed.

I tried to make myself appear meek, frightened.

Rune pulled me closer to him. "Busy. What do you need?"

"They found Maven. Dead. In *her* cell." The guard looked from Rune to me and back again.

"What exactly are you implying?" Rune sneered, leaning in just enough to be intimidating.

The guard's eyes widened. "You were both clearly elsewhere, but Maven was burnt." Again, the guard's eyes drifted to me, the fire witch.

Rune pulled me close. "As you said, we were otherwise occupied. What else is it that you want?"

Suitably cowed, the guard now kept his eyes on his feet. "Galwick has called for you to meet him."

Rune was already starting to pull me away from the guard, acting so very like Landon, who was always an ass to anyone he thought below him.

Another wave of self-loathing hit. *What had I been thinking?* Watching Rune pretend to be my former lover just made it all hit home so hard.

Over his shoulder Rune shot, "Where?"

"His quarters."

As we moved away from that guard, Rune muttered. "That's in our favor. Where we need to go is near his quarters. But I don't like knowing that is where he is."

He led me down one of the many staircases in the castle. Galwick's quarters were up a few floors. He could sift there. Rumors said no one else could, other than his closest guards.

"Can we sift?"

Rune shook his head. "*I* could, but not Landon." But then Rune's lips pursed in thought. "Well, maybe he could now. I can't risk it either way. And Wall, I rarely used that privilege. I never knew what I might find myself in the middle of."

I pulled a face, not knowing what he referred to. Orgies? Torture? Frankly, I didn't want to know.

We climbed and climbed. Guard's would see him, raising a finger to get his attention, but Rune with Landon's face would just wave them away with an, "I know. Already heard. I'm on my way."

I tried to hide my nerves, but thankfully, no one would think otherwise.

"We're nearing the alcove..."

Guards swarmed the hall. How would we manage to go wherever he wanted us to go?

Rune's hand on my arm tightened. "Create a distraction."

A torch was lit far down the hallway. Guards ran back and forth. If I made that explode, it'd surely get their attention.

I kept my head down, harnessing the fire, testing it. I let it spark a few times, which earned a few shouts. Last thing I wanted was for them to suspect a witch, but a flame sparking wouldn't do much.

"On my mark, explode that thing," Rune whispered. "We're a few steps away."

Ahead, I saw no one on either side of the hall.

"Now."

I unleashed the flame. A loud boom reverberated down the hall, vibrating the floor. That maybe was more than I had meant...

Rune turned our backs to the Wall, facing the commotion. Guards lay scattered on the floor, and a gaping hole punched through the wall the torch had hung on. As guards switched directions, all running to the sound screaming, "Protect Lord Galwick!" Rune stepped us back through the wall behind us.

A glamour, again. I should've known. Galwick was certainly fond of them to hide all his secrets. Rune turned us about. We were in a narrow corridor. His shoulders brushed the edges. "Now we run."

Rune led the way as we hoofed it down the secret tunnel. The shouting from where we had been gradually quieted, but the castle alarms continued and began ringing in a pattern. I knew that one. It called everyone to arms.

"I hope you know what we're doing."

Rune let out a slightly maniacal laugh. "I wasn't quite expecting a hole in that wall, but it certainly got their attention."

I desperately wanted to know how we were going to get out. This tunnel held no offshoots. I felt like I was being herded. But for all I knew, there were glamours every few feet.

The tunnel descended.

"What is this?"

"An absolute-shit-is-flying-everywhere escape plan for Galwick." Again he laughed, and I felt like I was missing out on the joke.

A stench like I've never smelt before in my life permeated the air. Growing only stronger as we ran.

Feces.

Lots of it.

A river of it.

"The sewers that lead out of the castle."

Cobblestones lined the floor, the walls. All of them were slicked with moisture. A canal in the center flowed with raw sewage. But nowhere was there a boat for Galwick.

But Rune's shadows spooled out of him on top of the brown, frothy excrement. He stepped in it, wobbled, extended a hand to me.

I didn't want to do it, but what choice did I have?

"We'll keep this as pleasant as we can, but we may have to get out into it at some point."

"Oh Wall." I swallowed the bile threatening to creep up.

The shadow boat he'd crafted held.

"Only possible, thanks to your power boost."

Together we sat down, and the boat drifted into the center. I held a hand to my nose, but that only helped so much.

I knew he waited to just be outside of the castle to sift us. Those damn wards.

The tunnel made a hard turn, and a roaring noise echoed.

"That doesn't sound good," I said.

"It's the main way Galwick keeps anyone from trying to enter this way."

Underneath us, Rune's shadows disintegrated. And we both plunged into the sewage water. It was frigid and rank, and it was everything I could do to keep it out of my mouth.

Rune's arms found me, pulled me close. I was just about to ask him what the heck happened when a voice rang out.

"You thought I wouldn't figure it out? Stupid boy. Shield him!"

Rune's head rocked back, and I gripped on to him, my head whipping around, trying to figure out what was going on. Blast this cold, wet tunnel. I'd have to dig so deep to find flame.

Bonds of air whipped around us and plucked us out of the filthy water, dropping us at the side.

And now I saw who it was. Galwick. Accompanied by Landon, a witch I'd never liked, and the Oracle bound and gagged. And just behind them, something shimmered. The wards that encompassed Galwick's castle.

Rune shook his head like he was coming to.

The Oracle's head hung down. Air bonds must have had him propped up in a kneeling position.

Galwick strode forward, pointing his sword at Rune's throat, tipping his chin up. "Did you think it would be so easy?"

I glanced at Landon, whose shirt was bloodied down his side. The stain ran all the way down his leg. A kidney shot. How'd he live?

A sick feeling settled into me. If he lived through that, then Galwick had taken extreme measures. Even fae with their superior self-healing abilities or life-witches couldn't bring someone back from the dead.

The other witch's eyes were fastened to Rune's chest. She shielded his source. Other than being loosely held by Landon's air bonds, no one paid me any mind. So I began searching for fire. I was tired from earlier, but I could do something even if it was only a surprise to break the witch's concentration. Rune had so much behind that shield that once he was free...

"What did the Oracle and that witch send you to do?" Galwick pushed forward a bit and Rune swayed back.

The Oracle's head swung up. They'd gouged out his eyes, blood smeared down his cheeks. "Don't tell them! Let them kill me."

Galwick smiled. "Oh, I don't plan on killing you. I plan on taking your soul."

The Oracle visibly paled. "You...you," he stammered, "can't do that."

"Ah, but you see, that stone you stole." Galwick flicked his gaze back to Rune and I. "Wasn't *the* stone of Cirrelea, at all. Why would I leave that out so someone could steal it?"

Rune and I exchanged a glance. We had to get that stone.

The Oracle shouted, "He's lying, he has to be. I tested that stone! He must have taken some serum!"

A serum. Because fae can't lie.

I kept digging outward, toward the castle. The castle had torches, fires, something I could harness, and I didn't have to send my witchery through solid rock.

Galwick rifted a blue stone, held it in his hand.

"That...this cannot be," the Oracle muttered. To us he said, "I know what I tested. Finish the..." Galwick spun and clocked him on the head with the pommel of his sword.

"I know he was a father figure to you that I never was, but we have a chance now at healing that rift, Rune."

Rune laughed.

"You have a stone. I have a stone. Together, our power would be immeasurable."

"I thought the one I had was a fake," Rune said.

"Not quite. I said it wasn't *the* stone of Cirrelea. There are more than one. And when together, they are even more powerful."

Rune struggled a moment against Landon's air bonds. Growled.

Then asked. "Then why haven't you done anything with both of them until now?"

"Who says I didn't?"

I couldn't let this keep going on. And I was so close. I could almost feel the heat of a torch.

"What did you do?"

"Just some experiments. Some serums. I wanted to start small. But then they stole — you stole — the one and halted my progress."

Just a little further. Sweat broke on my brow, and thankfully with all the muck on me I doubted anyone could see.

"Always a thorn in your side, wasn't I? Couldn't stand I inherited your talent, too."

Rune kept him talking. The bond was blocked, but he somehow knew what I was doing.

Galwick laughed. "I put you to good use. And I'll put you to even better use if you hand over that stone."

"And why would I do that?"

Landon's air bond tightened around my throat, and I squeaked in surprise. I hung onto my witchery but lost a bit of distance. My hands clawed at my throat as I scrabbled for every inch more that I spooled out my witchery, reaching for that flame so tantalizingly close.

"You think I didn't know? I could smell you all over her as soon as she arrived. Maven figured it out. Fated mates." Galwick's eyes flicked between the two of us. "You'll do as I ask, or I'll let Landon do what he does best to her."

So close. Just an inch more.

Landon held the bond around my neck so tight that blackness pooled around the edges of my vision.

But then I had it.

Fire.

Warmth. Heat. Comfort.

And blazing hot revenge.

I lashed out with it. A whip of fire, hitting both fae and the witch.

Landon's air bonds dropped from me, and I sucked in a breath. My lungs burned.

Rune unleashed himself. Shadows as thin as garrotes sliced through the air in front of us. Landon however blocked himself with an air shield. Galwick did the same with a shield of shadows.

The witch, however, didn't fare well. Her body dropped to the ground in several pieces. A sickening thud of body parts.

Rune drew his sword, and at the same time sent some fae power to me. An invitation.

No hesitation. I met his thread with my witchery and molded it to my will. An air shield around Landon was a problem, but he didn't know what we could do.

He lashed out at me with whips of air, but he tired. Whatever they did to heal him hadn't given him his full power back. So I lashed out, melting the rock beneath him. No air shield could protect him from that, and like most arrogant fae, he hadn't considered it.

His body plummeted into molten rock, incinerating immediately.

Rune battled now with his father, who protected his feet with swirling shadows, having seen what I did to Landon.

So I did the only thing I could think of. I sent my witchery into Rune. He seized it, grinned, then became a blur of bodies and movement.

Galwick paused, seemingly dumbstruck by what Rune just did.

Rune's movement stopped, and the blur morphed, clarified and became copies of Rune, stepping around Galwick, surrounding him. And they all held their sword pointed at Galwick.

Galwick panicked, swirling around. His sword clanked on each sword held by a copy of Rune. He didn't know which one was real.

But I did. I could feel it, sense it. My witchery was with him.

Every image of Rune began to stab in, slowly. So slowly. Encroaching in on Galwick.

Galwick, in full panic mode, tried to slap each sword away. He wasn't even considering his power anymore.

A sword snaked in between the only barrier of defense Galwick kept: his swirling shadows.

With a quick stab, Rune struck Galwick through his heart. With a vicious twist to his sword, Rune made Galwick's shadows disappear.

He stalked around the body of his father before he kicked the body, to slide his sword out, only to hack of Galwick's head with one swing.

I didn't hesitate. I grabbed the head by the hair and tossed it into the sewage filled water where he belonged.

Rune came to me and we embraced. "Are you ok?"

His eyes caught on my throat. "I would have loved to do the honors of murdering that son of a bitch for you, but I have to say your way was quite satisfying."

The Oracle groaned and sat up, taking note of the surrounding carnage. "You can't stay here."

Rune and I exchanged a glance. I'd barely had a moment to think about what came next, but Galwick dead seemed like a net of safety for us.

"The crown has already passed to the next in line."

"Iolas..." Rune's gaze got a faraway look.

"He will hunt you down, just like his father. He's potentially already on the way. Quick. Get Galwick's stone."

Rune fished in Galwick's pocket. He'd never rifted it away, so sure of his own victory.

"We haven't finished the pages for the Summer Court," I said.

The Oracle only bobbed his head, "I know, my child. Vespa and I knew those would never be placed. But that is good. It is weaving the fate we want. Cross the Wall. Hide the stones. Protect them. They will be safe on the other side." He winced. "Relatively speaking."

But...but. "Doesn't a stone have to stay here?" I asked.

The Oracle smiled. "There is one more, and it is safe in a deep, dark place. But the fae here can't have the ability to join that one with more. The courts here have grown too much like what they hated. They have forgotten, willfully, what ages ago they forswore.

Dark times are ahead. So cross the Wall. And at least one fated pair may have a happy ending."

And with that, he produced something from a pocket at his chest and swallowed it.

Rune staggered back, eyes wide. "Oracle, no!" He lunged to hold the man, a father-figure, in his arms.

"What did he do?" I stood there, not knowing how to help.

Frothy saliva bubbled at the edges of the Oracle's lips as his body began to tremble.

"He took hemlock. A poison I used many times to great effect. Maven made it highly concentrated. It causes near instant death."

The Oracle's hand reached up to Rune's face. "I loved you as if you were my own as much as I could. Go now. Do this for me. Do it for Cirrelea. And be happy." His sightless gaze fell on me. "Vespa would say the same to you if she'd been given the chance."

His body went still, and his hand fell from Rune's cheek.

Rune placed the Oracle's body down with as much love and respect as one could before he leaned forward, kissing his cheek.

Standing, Rune outstretched a hand to me. "He's right. We have to go. Iolas will never stop. I apologize, but I'll have to sift us several times to hide our trail."

"Rune, I'm so sorry." I cast my gaze toward the Oracle, whose death would weigh heavy on him, ignoring his words..

Rune pulled me close. "I will miss him. He meant more to me than my actual family. Much more, but he's giving us a chance he never had with Vespa. One that Fenwyn fights for with Muriel. And for that, I will always be grateful, and I can't throw it away. We can't dally. Besides," he flicked his fingers, removing all the muck from both of us, before he tucked my hair behind my ear, "I want the rest of my life with you to begin as soon as possible."

He leaned in for a kiss. And this kiss was full of all his longing, his sadness, his joy, and the promise of a shared life and a shared bed.

"Then let's not wait," I said with a grin on my lips as I nipped at his lower lip. "And let's make them proud."

The world swirled out of view before we popped into the Spring Court near the Wall.

Rune placed a hand on my forehead, and a cooling seeped into me, easing my stomach.

"Ugh. Why didn't you do that before, you bastard?" I swatted him away.

Rune only chuckled as he took my hand and set off at a jog. "On day one? I had to conserve my power."

"You couldn't have spared even a bit?"

He smirked over his shoulder at me. "You were being such a brat. You kind of deserved it."

"I bet you could have made it so we didn't need to swim naked either."

He grinned, laughing as he ran. "You'll never know."

He swung me toward him, placing a kiss to my lips, then sifted us again.

"One more time for good measure, my love."

After a trip to the Winter Court and another jog, Rune sifted us to the Wall in the Summer Court. The cave where we should have left the last box.

The air was dry and warm. A creek burbled beside us. Birds tweeted. None of Galwick's or Iolas' men were here to stop us.

Something urged me to look at the journal. Rune rifted it in front of us. The next pages had filled with script. "Don't leave the summer box here. Take it with you."

The fae source appeared in Rune's grip, and we placed it inside one of the stones. I held it in my hand, curled against my chest while Rune held me close to him.

"We do this together," I whispered, a tremble going through me as I was about to leave my home and into the unknown.

"We'll do everything together from now on." He smiled, pulling our clasped hands to his lips and pressing a kiss to my knuckles. "I don't even care what is on the other side as long as I face it with you next to me."

A shout outside rang out. "I picked up a trail!"

Rune's fingers tightened. "I love you," he whispered as he walked us into the Wall.

"And I love you."

His face lit up, filled with a contentment I fully understood as we fell through the Wall and into the human lands.

The story of the foretold apocalypse continues with *So Fell Are the Fae*. Available now!

A hunted witch. A cursed fae lord. A dying land.

Innara thought she knew what it was to be hunted as a witch in a world of humans. But when she falls through the Wall into Faerie, land of her mortal enemies, she's quickly captured by a far more deadly foe.

Winter Court Lord, Kir, is ruthless and wastes no time imprisoning Innara in his dying court. Her pleas to go home are ignored. No one should be able to cross the Wall. However, he agrees to strike a bargain: a piece of her soul and the use of her strange magic to help solve the mystery of his decaying world in exchange for his help to find a way home.

But Innara isn't just a wayward witch—she's the greatest threat to his life.

She's his fated mate, the one creature who can kill the powerful immortal lord. Bound by a curse, Kir will never know true love's touch lest he surrenders his power to an opposing court. So he's forced to keep his mate at a distance while they race against time and enemies to save all of Faerie.

And she can never know.

So Fell Are the Fae is the first book in the Through the Wall trilogy. This slow burn, enemies-to-lovers fae fantasy is perfect for those who love fated mates, he-falls-first, witches, curses, angst, and lots of twists and turns.

About the Author

Kat grew up in the US and now lives in the Great White North with her husband and three children. Since she moved around a few times, her accent is kind of wonky, a little southern drawl with an 'eh' attached.

She's always wanted to be an author, but discovered her love for fantasy and romance in college at the used bookstore. Now she loves writing fantastical worlds with swoony romances just as much as she loves reading them.

Learn more and sign up for her newsletter at katkeenanbooks.com.